This book is dedicated to all those Rugby entertained me when I was a lad leaning on the the forties.

Time lends enchantment to memory. I recall Ernie Ashcroft and Ted Ward of Wigan, Alt Ward and Jack Kitching of Bradford, and Jimm... St. Helens favourite and great tactician. Those were the days of huge crowds. How often do we hear the cry to-day *"Don't go back to the cloth cap image!"* I would hazard a guess that most clubs would welcome the sight of fifteen thousand cloth caps on the terraces!

Our game is so different to-day from the game played in the thirties and forties; sophistication has spread its veneer over the sports image; money speaks in loud tones, we have sponsored teams, professional players and televised games; not to mention videos, substitutes, walkie-talkies, blood bins and road shows. Despite all these *'advances'* league is still a game of the people – whether they wear flat caps or not. It is the man on the terrace who makes the game.

Let us hope that the sport will spread in popularity and that once again the hordes will return to the grounds shouting on their favourites in good humoured banter.

We don't want the yobbos in our game but we do need 'verbal conflict' – good old northern 'lingo', terraces packed with 'comedians' – all having a go at the opposition and even the ref. He can stand it! The game is still a great spectacle. Our players are better and fitter than they ever were.

Let's get out on those embankments and into those stands to cheer them on!

Once again Joshua Hepplethwaite is back in harness. Thanks to the reception afforded 'Up t' Rovers,' my first R.L. novel, I decided to do a sequel. I hope you like it!

My thanks are due to Kevin Vose my son, who type-set the book; not forgetting my good friend Brian Parkinson for his cartoons.

Let Play Commence!

John D. Vose

John D. Vose
February 1994

Chapter 1

Bad News For Joshua

Joshua Parkinson Hepplethwhaite, to give him his Sunday name, was in a furious mood as he sat at the office desk of his mill in Bramfield. As a cotton mill owner he was used to lost contracts and fierce opposition from other mills. To lose any contract was always a setback. He had struggled to keep his head above water during the grim, stringent period of the early 'thirties. Now, with the decade drawing to a close, things had improved.

An upright, God-fearing man, he regularly thanked his maker that his work force had full employment. He dreaded having to lay workers off. His compassion for the unemployed was a direct result of his own experiences as a lad, back in the very early years of the century. That very morning he had received news that a very large order for sheets had been given to another mill. At fifty years of age Joshua could have afforded to have sold up and concentrated on his position as chairman of Bramfield Rovers Rugby League Football Club. Many a man in his position would have sold out for a colossal figure and gone off to enjoy himself. Not Joshua. He knew that if he did his workers' future would be in jeopardy. His doctor was always telling him to take it easy. The double strain of running a mill and being at the helm of a rugby league club had affected his health, especially his bladder, or 'waterworks', as they say in the north. If it wasn't one thing it was the other, he thought, as he gazed at the curtly typed letter before him.

'Bagworthy's Company do not require any further supplies of

sheets - - - - - '. Two years previously he had received letters from creditors and banks telling him that the game was up at the rugby club. It had been enough to drive a man to the verge of despair. Joshua had weathered the storm, the club had survived, and now they were in a respectable position in the league. At the time of the club's near demise the orders for sheets had been coming in regularly. But now the situation had been reversed. He would just have to go on the 'knocker' again, just like he had when starting the business as a young man canvassing for orders. He would start that very morning in his own town, then he would go off doing the rounds to get business. It had happened before, contracts lost and won, the ebb and flow of business, the good times and the bad.

He was a fighter both in business and in sport and still the foremost mill owner in the town.

'The Biggest Sheethouse in Bramfield' was his slogan.

To say he was very cross would be an understatement. He was *furious*. The fact that he had lost the contract annoyed him, of course, but it was the fact that it had gone to Barnacre Fabrics, a mill in Bruddersby just over the border in Yorkshire, that really incensed him.

Hadfield Barnacre was Joshua's arch rival in rugby league, the chairman of Bruddersby Stanley, a typical gritty Yorkshire side renowned for its tough forwards. It was always a battle when Rovers played Stanley, Yorkshire versus Lancashire, but the players never bore any grievances. They knocked heck out of one another on the field of play, but were the best of mates off it. Not so the chairmen. They fought like two tom cats whenever they met. On more than one occasion they had been warned by the Rugby League Council for bringing the game into disrepute.

Joshua rose to his full six feet in height and placed his corpulent backside in front of his fire. It was a wintery morning and icicles had woven an eccentric pattern on the office window.

"Would you like a nice cup of tea, Mr Hepplethwaite?" asked his secretary. Miss Hyacinth Grimshaw fussed around her employer as was her wont.

"I would an' all, Miss Grimshaw! 'Appen it'll warm me up."

"Shall I put a stick in it?"

"A what lass?"

"A stick,"

"A what lass?" he repeated.

"A stick, Mr Hepplethwaite. It's an old navy term, it means a drop of rum."

"Oh, in that case you can put a tree in it. I need summat to give me a lift."

When Miss Grimshaw was out of the office making the tea, Joshua burst into a fit of swearing.

"I'll swing for t'swine!" he roared. "I don't mind losing bloody contract but to lose it to that oily turd of all people. And what's more he's got on to the trail of Dai Powell and all my best kept secrets and he gets to know - - . - - I'll get to the bottom of this, I will 'an all - - - -. By gum, I'll turn over heaven and earth to find out."

Dai Powell was a welsh rugby union stand-off half who played for Cardiff. He was considered to be the hottest property in the amateur code. If it had been publicly known that Powell was a possible for the league ranks then the big clubs like Huddersfield, Wigan and Leeds would certainly have been in the field. As it was, Rovers' chief scout, Stanley Keighley, had made overtures to Powell who had in turn expressed a lot of interest in the club. Stanley was very optimistic that Powell would eventually sign professional forms. Rugby League is like a potent drug to some men. It was like that with Joshua Hepplethwaite. He would have gone through hell and high water for his beloved Rovers. Not that the spectators really appreciated his efforts, they were never satisfied unless the side won every week.

The supporters were constantly letting him know that they

needed a good stand-off. He had been very confident that he could land Powell. Now his confidence was shattered. Of course he knew that the opposition for the R.U. man's signature would be stiff, he'd never expected it to be easy. What infuriated him was that the news of the possible signing had been leaked to Hadfield Barnacre from his own club in Bramfield. There was an informer in the camp. But who was it? Who was the rotten apple?

When miss Grimshaw returned with the tea Joshua knocked it back with relish.

"By gum, Miss Grimshaw, that were reet good,"

He pulled on a thick crombie overcoat and placed his bowler hat firmly on his head. He was ready to face the cruel Bramfield winter weather. "I'm off to see if I can get some more work for t'mill, lass. Nil carborundum, as they say - - - - do not despair!"

As Joshua made his way along the icy cobbled pavements making his business calls he was rudely accosted on at least two

occasions by supporters dissatisfied with the team's mediocre performances. Bramfield folk didn't mince words. It was straight from the shoulder stuff.

"Our cat's a better stand-off than yon mon you've got playing theer", was the opinion of a gas lamp lighter busy replacing mantles in the street lamps; while a rag and bone man pushing a hand cart full of donkey stones called out "You couldn't run a chip shop you lot. I'd sack committee if I had owt to do with club, and let a monkey run it - - - - - can you spare a fag, mister, and 'appen a match an all?"

That's how it was in Bramfield. Speak your mind one second and all forgotten in the next. Joshua handed the man a woodbine. He was used to such talk. He had to be thick skinned. Besides, he'd survived when times were much harder at the club. All they really needed was a good out-half but they were like hen's teeth at the present time - certainly there were no good ones going begging. If only he could sign Dai Powell! It would be the sensation of the season. To think that snake in the grass Hadfield Barnacre was on his trail. How in hell's name did he get on to him? Powell had sworn to Stanley Keighley that he would give the Rovers the first refusal. He had insisted that they kept quiet about it as he was very concerned that Cardiff Rugby Union Club would get to hear of it. No, it couldn't be Powell who had spilled the beans. Joshua was convinced that it was an inside job. Worn out with worry over the lost contract and the added anxiety over the union half-back he eventually arrived home to his terraced house. Both he and his wife Phoebe Maude had no desire to live in the country. Joshua was rich enough to have joined his fellow mill owners as a resident of the Cheshire suburbs of Manchester. Many men from the mill went to work daily in the Lancashire mill towns but returned every evening to their homes.

Hence their nickname 'The Manchester Men'. Nobody could ever say that the Hepplethwaites were 'peas above sticks'. Although they had a bathroom and the luxury of a separate

W.C., old habits died hard with Joshua, who preferred to have a bath in a large zinc tub in front of a roaring coal fire.

Phoebe Maude complained every time he sat in the tub, and that evening was to be no exception as Joshua soaked after a hard day.

"Why you can't use the bathroom luv, I don't know. Water spills all over the lino. You look like an elephant sitting in a soup bowl."

"I like to do it the old fashioned way lass, like me dad and his dad before him. I've had 'leccy' put in and you've got a carpet in t'parlour, so I'm keeping up wi' modern times - - - - - I'll get you a maid if you want luv."

"Nay, Josh - - - - - I'm only joking lad - - - - - but if we did have one it would stop you bathing in front of fire - - - - - I'm content lad but I'm worried about you. You're driving yourself too hard, why don't you sell up and concentrate on your rugby league? And while we're on the subject why don't we go for a

Joshua in his zinc tub in front of the fire. Note the bowler hat. It was not worn for sartorial effect but as a safe place for the soap

early holiday - - - - - we don't have to wait while Wake's Week do we? A few days in a good hotel in Lakes an' plenty o' fresh air will do you good. You must look after yourself luv."

Joshua just grunted.

"Draw the blinds luv, I want to dry mesel - - - - I could eat a scabby cow between two Ribble buses. How long will tea be lass?"

"Four inches, it's a sausage," replied his wife.

"I'll fettle thee when I get dry," laughed Joshua.

He knew he was lucky having a wife like Phoebe Maude. She was very easy going. She never knew the moment he'd be away on Rovers' business. Many a time they had cancelled trips out when Joshua had been called to attend to urgent matters. Phoebe Maude had another reason to be cheerful. It was Wednesday night and the weekly trip to Bramfield Hippodrome lay ahead after tea. After a good knife and fork 'tuck in' of tripe and onions and barm cakes they were ready for the second house.

"By the heck, that were a reet good tea, luv," said Joshua. "You can't beat barm cakes to soak up tripe juice - - - - - I'm glad I didn't marry one o' them southern women you hear about who feed their husbands on lettuce and spring onions every day. That's alright for rabbits but it's no good for a working man - - - - - who's on the bill tonight luv? I've forgotten".

"Fancy forgetting George Formby! And there's your favourite turn on, *Andreanny the Yodelling Tramp*. Then there's *Two Ton Tessie O'Shea, Little Tweet the Canary Caruso, Lulu and her Singing Snakes, Troise and his Mandoliers*, and *Nugent's Naughty Nudes in Daring Scenes from the Orient."*

"By the hecky thump! What a bill!" said Joshua in gleeful anticipation.

As the couple entered the foyer of the theatre Phoebe Maude remarked "Well there's one person we won't be seeing, Joshua, that's for sure,"

"Who's that luv?"

"Who's that? Why, Mary Alice Postlethwaite of course."

"What's up with her?"

"What's up with her? She's dead, crate egg!"

"Ee, I'd forgotten luv — no disrespect meant,"

"It were a big funeral, Hadfield Barnacre were at it,"

Joshua's ears burned at the mention of his rival.

"What were he at it for?"

"He was a cousin of sorts — didn't you know? She was related to Jeremiah Crumpsall as well. Crumpsall and Barnacre are related as you know - - - -."

"You what? I didn't know! What's the relationship?"

"Jeremiah is Hadfield's brother in law - - - - don't you know anything? Are you on this earth or Fullers? Your mate Stanley Keighley was the undertaker. It was all over the local paper. Of course, *you* only read the rugby league reports don't you?"

"Nay lass, I'm not that bad - - - - so that's it! It's all come plain now. I think I'm getting the picture lass."

"What's up with you Joshua? What are you rabbiting on about? You've got a yed full o' jolly robbins, as me dad used to say."

In answer he gave Phoebe Maude a big kiss on her cheek.

"What's that for luv?"

"For making a knotty problem very clear. Come on luv, let's enjoy t'show - - - I'm looking forward to that yodeller and I'm going to buy you the biggest ice cream cornet they've got. Then on way wom we'll stop at Seth Hardbottle's fish and chip emporium for a fish supper - don't say as I don't look after you, Mrs Hepplethwaite!"

"Ee, by the cram, you do an' all, Joshua. Even though your thoughts are on rugby league most of time, you're a good hearted chap. A bit daft but good hearted. I could have done worse, I suppose."

She gave Joshua a hearty kiss on his lips which made him splutter with embarrassment. Such affectionate exhibitionism was looked upon with raised eyebrows amongst the working class of northern England.

Jeremiah Crumpsall, chairman of Bramfield town council, had two pet hates in his life. One was scrum halves, the other was Joshua Hepplethwaite, the chairman of Bramfield Rovers Rugby League club.

The first hate is explained by the fact that his wife ran off with a Salford half-back. The second one can be traced to the fact that Joshua was everything Jeremiah was not; the rugby league man was jovial, popular, and as honest as the day is long. The two men had clashed many a time at council meetings, usually over the Rovers. Jeremiah was a sanctimonious man, and a hypocrite, and Joshua had told him so on more than one occasion. He was the typical pharisee. He loved to be seen to be doing good; to be observed being a stalwart Christian at church functions. However, he did not like to be observed watching *Nugent's Naughty Nudes* when they appeared at Bramfield Hippodrome, although he openly campaigned for the moral protection and cultural welfare of chorus girls on the music halls. Certain people had accused him of being associated with the halls for reasons other than cultural ones. Joshua had called him a mucky old man to his face, his candour only serving to increase Jeremiah's animosity.

This evening Jeremiah was sitting in a box wearing a wig and a pair of dark glasses. At the interval he was at the bar downing a double gin and 'it'. As president of the United Churches Temperance League one would have hardly expected him to be propping up a bar. But nothing Jeremiah did surprised Joshua.

"Good evening Jeremiah, enjoying the show are we?" asked Joshua, relishing the situation.

"I think you are mistaking me for someone else," was the curt reply.

"Oh, I don't think so, I'd know thee anywhere, Jeremiah. We've had many a fall out, me and thee, and we've both made it plain we hate each other's guts. Well, I've got one more little bone to pick with thee - - - - - you call yourself a loyal citizen of Bramfield, born and bred in the town, yet you're hand in glove with Hadfield Barnacre of Bruddersby Stanley, and what's more you're trying to help him pinch a rugby union star from under us noses. Your name should be Judas, not Jeremiah."

"I didn't come here to be insulted, Joshua Hepplethwaite," said Jeremiah in a low tone, trying not to attract attention.

"Oh, where do you usually go, then? So now you know me, do you?"

"If you want to discuss a private matter kindly make an appointment to see me in the council chamber. You know the procedure, you were on t'council"

"Bollocks," said Joshua angrily, "private matter is it? It's the business of every decent citizen of Bramfield, of every loyal supporter of the Rovers. Our club has risen from the ashes, like Felix from the depths of despair. From financial death, to once more being a leading team in the league. You and your council pals wanted to close us down, didn't you? You're more interested in replacing piss oils in t'park and stocking lake with carp and roach, than you are in the town team. Well, you've gone too far this time Jeremiah - - - - I'll have thee shown up for a traitor proper this time, you wait and see. I know summat and you don't know I do - - - so there, me owd cock. Put that in your pipe and smoke it."

"Oh, do enlighten me, Joshua," Jeremiah's remark was acute with sarcasm.

"Hadfield Barnacre is your brother in law!" Jeremiah's face fell visibly. Even his wig slipped over his left ear. He was saved from more embarrassment by the ringing of the bell for the second half of the performance.

"Second half about to begin, ladies and gentlemen!" bawled the bar steward "George Formby's on in second half."

Joshua pointed to his adversary. "You prefer *Nugent's Naughty Nudes*, don't you Jeremiah?"

Sniggers from the drinkers in the bar greeted Joshua's remark.

"He looks a proper stage door Johnny, does that fellow," said a woman making no attempt to keep her voice down. Jeremiah gave Joshua a dirty look. "I'll swing for thee, Joshua Hepplethwaite," he murmured, as he sloped off back to his seat.

Joshua gave a sixpence to the barman.

"Here, lad, have a couple of pints on me. I've just told that snake in the grass off, and it's made me feel much better. You're a supporter of the Rovers, aren't you lad?"

"I am 'an all, mister," replied the barman eagerly.

"When are you going to get a new stand-off?"

"Oh, bloody hell, don't you start!" bellowed the chairman as he headed for his seat.

Chapter 2

The Supporters' Club 'do'

The ladies' section was a thriving one at the Rovers. Before the concert began a bring and buy sale was in full swing. Home-made rhubarb and ginger jam, Chorley cakes, 'jammy dodgers', Eccles cakes, parkin, cinder toffee and bottles full of sticky Uncle Joe's Mint Balls were in great demand, as were such northern favourites as potato pie, elderberry wine, and packets of tripe bits which were considered to be the tastiest morsels of all by old folk in Bramfield. Not to be outdone by all this home produce the 'Cockle King', who stood on Bramfield market almost everyday of his life, was threading his way through the assembled supporters with a tray full of sea food delicacies shouting: "Get yer cockles - fresh from Southport!"

The stall selling home made boiled sweets was doing even better business. Sucking a boiled sweet has long been a good old northern custom and most rugby league die-hards took a bag full with them to the match. Why, it was almost unknown in those days to stand on a terrace in Yorkshire, open to the vagaries and ferocity of a Pennine driven gale, without a bag of winter warmers - 'Owd Betty Plants' being a particular favourite. Never wrapped of course - wrapped 'uns were for cissies.

"Get the ale in lads!" The supporters' club members were true sons of suction. They would have supped a reservoir dry if it contained Seth Ogden's best bitter. Ogden's had supplied a free barrel of their 'Celebration Brew', so named because they had made it to celebrate Rovers winning the rugby league cup back in 1932. 'Owd Seth Ogden' as he was known locally, had negotiated a special price with the *Stoat and Trumpet* pub in Bramfield town centre so that the licensee could offer a halfpenny off every pint for the Rovers' supporters' club annual hot pot and concert. Bramfield, being a mining area, as well as a cotton textile town, had some of the best 'ale cans' in the north of England. Mild beer was the common tipple of the working man in those days, but with best bitter at five pence three farthings a pint against the usual sixpence halfpenny, it was getting a 'reet thumping' from the crowd who thronged the club room above the pub. Ha'penny barm cakes with hot dripping were selling as fast as the ladies' section could produce them.

"Order please! - - - Order please! - - -Belt up, can't you! - - - - -Order please! You're like a pack o' bloody wild animals - - - - order please! I've seen better behaviour from a ruddy kindergarten."

The president of the club, Samuel Ogglebottom, was shouting as hard as his lungs would allow. Gradually the crowd settled into their seats facing a wooden podium upon which stood a piano and an anaemic aspidistra with drooping brown leaves.

"Have you all got enough ale? - - - Reet, it's my duty and privilege as president of the Bramfield Rugby League Supporters' Club to introduce you to Mr Albert Heneberry, our worthy club chairman, who has brought along his concert party to entertain us. During the evening raffles will be held and we ask you to be as generous as you can - - - remember folks, the club's only as good as it supporters. We want Rovers to get back to them glory days, don't we - - - -?"

There was a thunderous reply by way of clapping, shouting and whistling.

Madam Alcari entertains the Rovers supporters club at it's annual 'do'.

"Of course we do!" yelled Samuel through the megaphone. "And now on wi' show!"

Albert Arbuckle Heneberry was a town councillor who had fought tooth and nail along with Joshua Hepplethwaite to keep the club afloat during the bad days. He was a Rovers man through and through. In the council chamber he was renowned for his wit, particularly for making crude remarks, and had often been sent to the 'Green Room', the council equivalent of the modern day 'Sin bin', by Jeremiah Crumpsall, the council chairman. A die-hard supporter, he would have followed Rovers through hell and high water, even to Widnes on a foggy day. When the fog and chemical fumes combined over the River Mersey it was a place to avoid. Great globules of floating chemical muck hung in the air and a foul stink contaminated the atmosphere. It must be said, however, that such horrors were not the sole priority of Widnes, pollution by industry was the order of the day in northern towns in days gone by.

Albert had made his brass out of constipation, being the heir to the Heneberry fortune amassed by Moses Obadiah Eli Heneberry who had invented and patented Heneberry's Do-It-Yourself Enema Machine. He boasted that it was even used by cannibal chiefs in deepest Africa. Moses Obadiah had rivalled that other great Lancastrian Beecham in keeping northern folk in motion. Now retired from his chemist's sundries business Albert had plenty of time to travel round the district with his concert party 'The Dinky-Doos'. Resplendent in a green smoking jacket with a red spotted dicky bow, Albert was introducing the first act of the evening - a woman of colossal stature; she would have dwarfed the biggest forward in the league. My powers of description are too inadequate by far to fully capture in words the raw boned appearance of this female colossus. Think of Emosi Kiloto and multiply by two.

"And now, lads and lasses, we have Madame Isolde Rubena Alcari, virtuoso of the musical saw. She's a Wigan lass but she can't help it, someone's got to be born there - poor sods. It's a grand instrument is the saw. You can play a saxophone but you can't cut firewood with it, can you? For her first item Madame Alcari will play for your delight the *Poly Nase* by Chopping followed by a selection from the opera by Mascara, *If she wants to wriggle let her.*"

Madame Alcari gave Albert a withering look. She was sick to death of his stupid prattle. Born Ada Gumstone near Ince, she had played her saw on the music halls for a quarter of a century until old Father Time had called her in to entertain locally. Gingerly placing a lace handkerchief beneath one of her many chins, she placed her bow on the saw and produced lovely music which very soon commanded complete silence in the club room. Only the sound of the odd belch broke up the spellbound silence. At the conclusion of her performance she was greeted with thunderous applause as well as some irreverent remarks.

"Get her signed on, Albert lad!" and "She's another Ken Gee

is that lass!"

The supporters were enjoying a traditional evening's entertainment provided by an institution which was one of the back bones of northern social culture. I refer to the concert party. In those days long before television became a regular feature in the home the wireless reigned supreme for those who could afford the luxury. A night out at the local variety theatre was a great treat, so was a night at the 'flicks', but one of the most popular forms of escapism was the home spun semi-professional concert party. Most towns had up to half a dozen, the members were in the main local people who had a flair for entertaining and were glad to earn a pound or two singing songs or reciting a monologue. These groups of entertainers performed in pubs, in church halls, old barns and village halls. The star of the party was usually the tenor, a plump rubicund man with a purple nose caused by reaching for too many high c's. It could equally have been a surfeit of local mild or bitter, for most artistes were fond of a 'sup'. Adorned with carnations in their button holes these gentlemen sang of love and war, the open road, gardens filled with roses and broken promises - victorian ballads often referred to as sentimental slush but with beautiful lyrics and melodies that have lived on to this day. The female vocal armoury was usually provided by a big beefy contralto or a demure soprano.

Instrumental diversion could be by a vocalist or a one string fiddle player, but the most popular entertainment of all during the 'thirties was the piano accordion or 'squeeze box', as it was known. No party was complete without a comedian of course, who always finished his act with a comic song.

Such was the fare being served up by the 'Dinky-Doos' concert party in the club room of the *Stoat* and *Trumpet* public house. The laughter and enjoyment was a reflection of the better times being experienced by the working class folk in the industrial towns. Not that life was a bed of roses. Far from it, but by 1938 times had eased. The great depression was wearing thin, the long dole queues had grown less, fun and games were once more providing good medicine to the tens of thousands who had suffered from the odious diseases of poverty and unemployment. Two years previously men had been laid off in their thousands in this area of Lancashire. You could have smelled the despair and degradation in Bramfield. To make matters worse the Rovers team had almost folded under the immense financial burdens of running a club. The old club had nearly succumbed to the death knell of bankruptcy, only to be saved in almost miraculous fashion two years later. Now they were holding their own in the league table and proving a thorn in the sides of many far more fashionable clubs.

Little did any of the happy supporters in the club room realise that a maniac in Germany was stirring up hatred and planning to overrun Europe. How could they? If someone had prophesied that rugby in the town would cease in two years' time, he would have been branded a fool.

With the concert in full swing it was now the turn of the accompanist to entertain in his dual role of monologuist. Although the item was a humorous one the laughter it drew was exaggerated by the fact that he had forgotten to remove his bicycle clips. When he was seated at the piano no one had noticed. Albert was seated on a high chair close to the artistes' podium, and before the next act he drained a whole pint pot of Ogden's bitter to cheers from the auditorium.

"By the gum, this ale's thin!" he remarked.

"Thy'd be thin if thee'd come up same pipe as that ale Albert!" shouted his stooge from the audience. Although it got a laugh a man on the front row shouted "Change the script, Albert owd cock. Frank Randle's been cracking that gag for centuries!"

Not to be deterred Albert started on a joke " - - - - there were this young lad - - - - - bohemian type he were, long hair down his back. Looked more like a woman than a chap. He were in t'barbers having an hair cut. Barber says 'I see you went to Manchester Grammar, lad.' 'How do you know?' asked the lad. "Easy," said the barber, "I've just found thee cap.'"

As Albert was on the point of introducing the next artiste, two chaps worse for ale started to slow hand clap. This was taken up by their mates behind who started to chant *"When are we getting a stand-off?"* Eventually, after Samuel Ogglebottom had yelled at them through his megaphone and threatened them with dismissal from the supporters' club, Albert was able to speak.

"All reet - - - - I know the unrest there is in the town over the fact that we need an out-half but they don't grow on trees. The directors are doing their best - - - -"

This was greeted with derisive boos and foot stamping.

"They couldn't run a bloody chip shop!"

"They're only in it for what they can make!"

A red headed man with cauliflower ears and no teeth stood up waving his fist in anger.

"That Joshua Hepplethwaite's only in it for his own ends," he yelled. This made Albert see red.

"Cut that out, do you hear me, young man? Mr Hepplethwaite is the best chairman any club could have. He's a Rovers man through and through is Joshua. His health has suffered over all the worry he's had over t'club - - so just moderate your opinions or I'll have thee out on thee lug 'oil. Think on! The club do need a good stand-off. We all know that. Only recently they tried to get Frank Tracey from St. Helens Recs. but Saints beat us to his signature. Mr Keighley, our chief scout..."

"Who's always pissed," interrupted 'red head'.

"As I was saying before I was so rudely interrupted," went on Albert, "Mr Keighley is constantly looking out for new talent on his travels and it is now not beyond the bounds of possibility that before long the club will sign a prominent welsh half-back to plug the gap. Just give 'em time. Now, can we get on with the entertainment? Presenting to you all the way from Oldham, a very good act - the only man who can juggle a pound of wet tripe whilst balancing a sack of ferrets on his head - Fred

Bloggs and Ada!"

On the completion of this novelty act it was time for the hot pot supper which was served by the ladies' committee. When all concerned had eaten their fill Albert called the assembly to order.

"It's now time for t'raffle lads and lasses. We need brass at club. First we need two new pigeons. As most of you will be aware the reporters at the match send their reports to their papers by carrier pigeon - two of our feathered carriers are getting the worse for wear. One of 'em ran into an eagle or summat big and he's flying backwards now, so he'll have to go. The other refuses to fly in the direction of Yorkshire so the reporter from the *Yorkshire Post* can't send his report."

"Why the 'ell don't they get a telephone!" yelled 'red head'.

"We've only got one phone in t'club," explained Albert, "they're all trunk calls and you've got to wind handle ten minutes before you can get t'operator to answer. It would take hours to get through to all the papers. The pigeons would be there and back by then. I don't reckon t'phone's all it's cracked up to be."

"You can have our budgie, Albert," yelled Samuel through his loud-hailer.

"Is it a homing budgie, Sam?" laughed Albert in reply.

"The other reason we need brass is to pay the unemployed men who help with the brassieres when the ground is frosty - we need your *support...* Do you get it? Bra's... support...?
To help with *t'Braziers* I should have said. So dig deep, folks - first prize is a packet of pork chops and second a stand ticket for t'next first team game. And now it is my pleasure to present to you our baritone, Mr Charles Muxworthy, who once sang with the Carl Rosa Opera Company. He's got a fine voice and you've a treat in store... I'm sure a lot of you remember *The Maid of the Mountains* playing at Bramfield Hippodrome when t'local amateurs put it on. Well, here's the best song from the show - *A Bachelor Gay.*"

Charles Muxworthy had such a powerful voice that all chatter was soon silenced as he attacked this rollicking song with panache and enthusiasm, the choruses being sung with great enjoyment by the audience who were urged on by Albert waving his gavel like Sir Hamilton Harty at the promenade concerts at Manchester Free Trade Hall.

'A Bachelor gay am I,
though I suffer from Cupid's dart,
but never I vow will I say die,
in spite of an aching heart.

For a man always loves a girl
or two, the fact must be confessed,
he always swears the whole way through
(to every girl he tries to woo)
that he loves her far the best
that he loves her by far the best (reprise)'

"Come on folks, loosen your elastic, altogether now!" shouted Albert, waving his gavel. The audience launched their vocal resources into the song's rollicking chorus:

'At seventeen he falls in love quite madly,
with eyes of tender blue
At twenty four he gets it rather badly
with eyes of a different hue

At thirty five you find him flirting sadly
with two or three or more
when he fancies he has passed love.
Its then he meets his last love
and he loves her as he's never loved before

A girl as you heard of old
is a kind of a paradox
She changes her mind more times I'm told
than even she does her frocks

For a man's like a moth around a flame
though it's nearly always found
He burns his wings, but all the same
the nicest part of Cupid's game
is fluttering round and round_ _ _
All together ladies and gentlemen!'

At the end of the song the audience yelled "Encore! Encore!"

"Never mind that, let's have some more!" shouted a solitary voice, to great amusement.

Charles Muxworthy knew how to handle an audience and gave them that great old northern favourite *'Don't go down the mine Daddy'*, followed by *'Alice where art thou?'* a great favourite with victorian ballad lovers. The audience once again joined in the choruses with gusto and Albert did a dance with an imaginary partner as he led the singing.

Without further ado he called on a pair of clog dancers who brought the house down as they danced away to the accompaniment of a piano accordion and a one-string fiddle.

To finish off the evening Albert introduced his ace - *'Happy Harry Hopwood, the man with the merry quips'*.

The ale continued to flow, meat pies and mushy peas with mint sauce were handed round - replete with good beer and 'gradely chuck', the Bramfield supporters enjoyed one of their best ever nights. Albert Heneberry was a contented man. The raffle had been a success. There was enough in the kitty to buy two new pigeons and something left over to give the brazier men a few coppers. In the morning he would report to Joshua Hepplethwaite, not forgetting to pass on the comments about the need for a new stand-off.

Ogden's best bitter, known as 'singing ale' in the town, had certainly taken effect, the 'sons of suction' had 'supped some ale toneet' as good old Frank Randle, the Wigan comic, used to say. The cobbled streets were alive to the sound of joviality, several young fellows in clogs did a dance in the town hall square to the accompaniment of a mouth organ and comb and paper, while Fred, the cow heel man, sold more pies than he'd done for years at his late night stall outside the knacker's yard. A good night had been had by all.

Chapter Three

Joshua's hopes are shot down

On first sighting Hadfield Barnacre, chairman of Bruddersby Stanley, the casual observer could be forgiven for thinking that he was a friend to all men, and a warm-hearted man of the people. Hadfield had a perpetual smile on his face, often an outward sign of inward warmth, but it was a falsehood. Stanley's chairman was not noted for love of his fellow man, his aim in life was to be successful and to hell with everyone else. His domineering ways and determination to succeed had made him a very prominent figure in rugby league circles, serving on the governing council at Leeds. Most people mistrusted him, and a great many hated his guts. He was certainly not a favourite with the players. He used people and basked in the glory obtained through other people's efforts. Other directors were very wary of Hadfield. Many were actually frightened of the man. Like a lot of bullies in this world, he didn't like it if you stood up to him. The man to do that was his rival chairman, Joshua Hepplethwaite. 'Owd' Josh, as he was affectionately known, was 'as soft as me cap', but wasn't the man to bow the knee to a little dictator like Barnacre. It was common knowledge that the two chairmen hated each other, and were rivals in business and in sport.

Hadfield's chauffeur parked the large Daimler on the director's car park while his employer made his way to the official's entrance. His round red face was reminiscent of a plump, ripe cherry in which cold, fish-like eyes lurked. His small rotund body waddled like a duck as he walked up the cinder to the grandstand. His co-directors, on away match duty, were already in the stand, having come with the players in the team's red charabanc. Hadfield was in his twentieth year with Stanley, and one of the very few chairmen who had travelled to away games on a horse drawn wagonette. He gave a general wave to all and sundry as he took his seat in the visiting directors' box. Armed with a thick rug to put over his knees and a brandy flask to keep him warm inside, he snuggled deeply into his brown camel coat and surveyed the familiar scene before him. Bramfield town brass band were setting up their instruments, and 'early doors' spectators were filing into the ground from various turnstiles, their breath rising like fog in the rarefied air.

"There's more holes in this stand than a colander," he remarked to one of his co-directors.

"It'll warm up when big mouth turns up," was the reply. Hadfield gave a thin laugh, and grinned at this reference to Joshua Hepplethwaite.

Joshua had called an emergency meeting of the directors for immediately before the game. Unlike most clubs in the league, Bramfield only boasted three directors. The Kearsley brothers, Bert and Bob, were long-standing officials of the club. In order to make ends meet, the club had dispensed with both secretary and treasurer. Bob Kearsley had taken over the paperwork, and Bert was in charge of the finance. Bob, known as 'Pickle

Kearsley' to most people in rugby league, was gazing out of the pavilion window at the scene before him. His beloved pickle jar stood prominently in the middle of the committee table. As he waited for the other directors to arrive, his eyes took in the disrepair and shabbiness of the ground. The two grandstands badly needed reboarding and at several locations the terracing was subsiding. The habit of the male supporters of urinating where they stood had contributed to this predicament, but it was no use trying to stop them, because the urinals in the ground were nothing short of medieval.

"Tuppence for your thoughts, lad." It was Joshua arriving with brother Bert.

"I were just thinking Josh, that if we had to do all the work on ground that this needs doing, there'd be nowt left for the players."

"Don't remind me, our Bob," said Bert, "as treasurer, I dream about these things. We haven't got much in the kitty, an' I'm afraid the ground will have to wait a little while. It's like being on top of Blackstone Edge, sitting in our grandstand. It's a beggar when you have to take a hot water bottle with you stuffed down your trousers, but if I didn't I'd be frozzen."

The three directors seated themselves at the table, and Bob handed round the pickle jar. After a good chew, Joshua opened the meeting. "Well, gentlemen, as the three of us know only too well, the eyes of the 'speccies' are upon us. If I go in chip shop or local pub, it's the same question. When are you going to get a new stand-off? Summat's got to be done, lads, it's no use playing other players in that position. We need a specialist. We've tried nearly all the backs there, but none of them are suited, but Bob here reckons Cowboy Smith will fit the bill, and as you know, he's in the team today. But with all due respect, I don't reckon as he's a stand-off."

"Give the lad a chance," said Bob, "Cowboy is one of the best attacking full-backs in the league. As you well know, most full-backs are kickers, but Cowboy can jink and swerve as good as anyone in the game."

"That's as mebbe, our Bob," said Bert, "we all know what he can do from full-back position, but can he do it at out-half? Is he a playmaker, like all good out-halves should be? It's one thing catching a ball at full-back and beating two or three opponents, but when you're getting ball fed to you from scrum it can be a different cup o'tea. I were only speaking to Cowboy yesterday when he were sweeping the street outside our office, and he told me he wasn't happy with the idea of playing out of position. Still, he'll do his best, I don't doubt, will lad."

"I'm sure he will," said Joshua, "but I'm adamant on one point, gentlemen. We'll see how he goes up to half-time, but if he doesn't show well, I'm going after the welsh lad. We've got to take bull by t'horns, Bruddersby Stanley are after him as well, and it's an early bird what gets the worm."

"What's the position then, Joshua?" asked Bob.

"Stanley Keighley has seen him play, and he reckons he's a natural for league. Now we all know our Stanley's a bit of a laddo, especially when he's been on the ale, but he has found us some good 'uns and he seems to have a genius for spotting welsh lads. But this lad,Dai Powell,isn't just a club player that Stanley's spotted, he's a proven player at international level, with three caps for Wales."

"It's the brass he wants what's worrying me," said Bert. "Five hundred quid is a lot of money. Will he definitely sign, or is he going to haggle for more, now that Bruddersby are in the frame?"

Joshua lit a large Havana cigar and puffed and blew as he answered. "Stanley has come to an agreement with him, that if we agree to five hundred, he'll sign. I reckon we ought to step in pronto. His club, Cardiff, are playing at Blackheath next Saturday, and me and Stanley are going down there to see him, and I hope to come away with his signature. Now gentlemen, are we agreed? Shall we go ahead?"

The two brothers looked at one another, Joshua gazed out of

the window and watched the terrace filling up behind the goal posts.

"We've got a good gate lads. Just think what we'll get when we have a new welsh international playing for us. It fetches them in droves from far and wide."

Bert Kearsley nodded. "All reet, if 'Cowboy' doesn't fit the bill by half-time, I'll agree Joshua. What do you say, Bob?"

"I'll go along with it," said Bob. "I only hope we're doing the right thing. At least Josh here will be able to go in his chippy without folks bothering him."

Joshua gave both of his co-directors a jovial slap on the back. "Come on lads, lets go to the grandstand, and think on; don't mention a word to Hadfield Barnacre about what we've been discussing. Have you filled the rubber hot water bottle? I might have to borrow it. It's like ruddy Siberia in that stand at times. I reckon as the club needs two hot water bottles Bert - can we invest in another?"

"Bring it up at next meeting, Josh lad," said Bert seriously.

"No wonder they call thee scrooge ... I bet 'Uddersfield directors have a bottle apiece."

"Aye, full o' whisky," laughed Bob.

When the Rovers officials were seated in the directors' box, next to their rivals from Bruddersby, the band struck up with a medley of hymns. This was a tradition at Bramfield, the original chairman and founder of the club had been a devout baptist, and even insisted on the players singing hymns at half-time. The crowd joined in as one man.

Onward Christian soldiers
marching as to war
with the cross of Jesus
going on before.

Christ the royal master, leads
against the foe:
forward into battle,
see, his banners go!
Onward Christian soldiers
marching as to war,
with the cross of Jesus
going on before.

At the sign of triumph
Satan's legions flee;
on then Christian soldiers,
on to victory.

Hell's foundations quiver
at the shout of praise;
brother's lift your voices,
loud your anthem raise.

After the hymns, the band did a marching routine in the centre of the pitch, before their usual sing-song medley of music hall numbers. This was the opportunity for a verbal punch-up between Hadfield and Joshua. The eyes of the best stand patrons were focused on the two chairmen. They knew they could never meet without a row. Joshua started the ball rolling.

"You'd never hear music like that in Yorksheer,"

"Rubbish. Brass banding is second nature in Yorksheer," said Hadfield, "and how the hell do you know, Joshua? What do you know about music?"

"How do I know? I'll have you know, Hadfield Barnacre, I were second cornet for Holroyd's tripe and trotter works for three year. We licked the pants off Yorksheer bands in contests. When did a Yorksheer band win at Belle Vue?"

"What about Brighouse and Rastrick and Black Dyke for 'evan's sake,?" countered Hadfield.

"There's always the odd exception, I'll grant thee. But generally speaking, Lancasheer is superior at wind instruments."

"Aye, and superior at wind-bagging - you're the best one at that, Joshua Hepplethwaite. I don't know about cornet, but you can certainly blow your own trumpet, Joshua lad. Like all Lancasheer folk, you're full o' wind and nowt else."

"There's some bad lots come out o' Yorksheer," said Joshua, ignoring Hadfield's jibe. "Did you know that the Kaiser had relatives in Heckmondwyke?"

"Don't talk rubbish, you'll be saying Attilla the Hun were a Yorksheer man next. Grow up Joshua, I've not come to indulge in childish banter with thee. 'Appen you're trying to take your mind off t'match. You're in for a good fettling today. 'Rough House' Reilly is back from injury, he'll sort you lot out. Best forrard in league."

"Aye, an' muckiest an' all," said Joshua.

"He never gets sent off," replied Hadfield.

"We've noticed that. How come, when he were with Broughton Rangers,he were sent off every other week? His missus used to have his tea ready for four o'clock, he never finished a match. Soon as he joins your club, he's a saint. Pure as the driven snow."

"What are you insinuating, Joshua?"

"Favouritism, that's what. You on council, an' all." Joshua waved a remonstrative finger at Hadfield.

"That's libel. Did you hear that?" He appealed to the listening stand ticket holders.

"Pardon me, gentlemen, but it's slander, not libel. It's only libel when it's written." Bert Kearsley enlightened them with a knowing nod to brother Bert.

"Some bloody consolation is that!" said Hadfield. "Call it what you like, it's no bloody compliment, an' I've made a mental note of it for future reference."

The veins on Hadfield's face were almost puce in colour.

"It's time for a sing-song," announced Bob. He was the best singer on the committee, and always led the community singing.

The band struck up a great favourite with the crowd, who joined in with great vigour.

"All together now!" bawled Joshua, as clutching the club hot water bottle he joined in with his fellow director.

'Daddy wouldn't buy me a bow wow
Daddy wouldn't buy me a bow wow
I've got a little cat
and I'm very fond of that!
but I'd sooner have a bow wow wow'

"All together now!" cried the bandmaster, leading the band into another chorus of the old favourite.

While Joshua and his board were joining in the singing, down below in the changing room the players were getting stripped for the match. Bruddersby always drew a large gate, for it was something of a derby match and to add extra spice it was Lancashire versus Yorkshire. The Bramfield changing room was no rose garden. Stale urine from the blocked-up toilets blended with wintergreen and horse liniment. A casual observer could have been forgiven for thinking that the game had been played already, for several Rovers men were having a shower. This was to wash away the coal dirt from their shifts at the pit face. Hard men who cared little for the toil they had put in down the mine, a good wash and they were fit and ready to do battle with the old enemy. Six of the team were miners, 'Cowboy' Smith was a street sweeper, several worked in local factories, while little Georgie Gardiner had the most unusual occupation of all. He was a professional crown green bowler, being employed by the Lancashire Professional Bowling Association, a member of an elite band of players who performed their skills on what was colloquially known as the 'Panel'. These were all-weather men, and even swept the snow off the green in order to play during winter-time. The game, which was run for the betting, was as northern as pie and peas and Wakes Week, full of colourful characters and wonderful bowlers who could have put touchers down on greens covered in rice pudding. From the Raikes Hotel at Blackpool to West 'Owton near Bolton, these men trundled their woods to eke out a living. George was a lucky man, at least he made his living in the open air. Only a proficiency at bowls had saved him from the hard labour of the coal mine. He was envied by all his team-mates. To make the occupational equation more bizarre, George worked as a 'knocker-up' in the early morning, before having a nap prior to his stint on the bowling green.

Willie Birch, the team's trainer, at this moment up to his elbows in rubbing oil, took bets at bowling matches, and travelled each day with George to the different venues. Little 'Woodbine Willie' Birch was one of those slightly seedy individuals we associate with horse-racing, shabby boxing gyms and long-distance spitting matches; the sort of character who wears a loud tie, a flamboyant tweed jacket and reeks of mild beer and camphor balls; a friend to all men while he is trying to put you on to a 'good thing', whether it be a boxer, a grey hound or a professional sprinter at Powderhall.

As Willie rubbed deeply into the calf muscle of 'Mucker' Casey's right leg, ash fell from his Woodbine into his liniment pot. Wilie had done more in his lifetime than most men could do in six, or so he said. Horses, boxers, wrestlers, rugby league players, they were all the same to him. He'd rubbed them all down in his time.

The Rovers captain was Ossie Evans, a centre, who had made his mark in the paid ranks in double-quick time. George Lewis, the old Saints captain and centre to the legendary Alf Ellaby, had recommended him. Back in his native South Wales, Lewis had spotted him playing for Llandyfuddyog, a minor club. No one had a better eye for a centre than George, himself one of the best ever to grace the hallowed turf of Knowsley road, and Joshua was very grateful to his old mate for the tip.

Ossie, like George himself, was no flyer, but it was his tactical play which endeared him to the crowd. Employed as a drayman at the local brewery, Ossie was well known to all the publicans, but being a strict teetollar it was of little advantage to him. In fact, he had become known as 'Bovril' Evans, due to his habit of requesting a cup of hot liquid when he had finished his delivery. Another pet hate of his was foul language. Ossie's views were well respected in the dressing room. When he had joined the club two years previously, the players trained twice a week, Tuesday and Thursday. Willie would get them to do two laps of the field, followed by ten sprints and a game of tick rugby. To finish off, there were no tactical talks and drawing board post-mortems, videos were a thing of the distant future, in fact, many players did not even have a wireless, never mind a television, an invention still very much in its pioneer stage. The players were expected to know the basics of the sport, such as tackling and passing. "Don't pass forrard - get stuck in! - get his bloody legs - he can't go beaat 'em - put it in back row when ref's not looking" (advice to scrum halves) were the gems of knowledge handed out by the trainer, who did everything from ordering the meat pies, re-studding the boots, to carrying the magic sponge in a bucketful of icy water.

Ossie had made changes, introducing a long run around the town and country lanes before training. He also got the players to reduce their intake of beer on the Thursday evening session after training. Some feat, to persuade a thirsty collier to cut down his ale ration, but Ossie did it and the team's fitness had improved.

But Willie had another function in the dressing room. Ossie always encouraged him to raise the players' spirits before a match. Certainly, Cowboy's Smith's spirits needed raising. As he sat on the bench he was dreading his stint as makeshift stand-off. He had told the directors that he didn't fancy the move from full-back, neither did Fred Turley, who was taking over 'Cowboy's' usual position. Ossie was a good psychologist, as well as a good captain and centre. He knew how to get Willie going, not that he needed any encouragement.

"Tell us about your adventures in the Orient, boyo," said Ossie, in his sing-song accent of the valleys.

"Ee, by gum, I had some rare times," said the ferrety little trainer, the perpetual Woodbine stuck between his lips. "I were engaged by a sultan to rub down his wives, the sultanas," he began.

"I bet it were *raisin'* you're temperature, Willie ... do you get it?" Bertie Fulton, a little Irish half-back, was the punner of the team, and his jest raised a stream of moans and groans, much to the delight of Ossie Evans, who could see his players beginning to relax.

"There were a few fruity pieces among them," said Willie to more groans. "But I'll tell thee how I got the job. I used to get a sporting paper called *Old Jonty's Guide to 'Orseflesh.* Some of the well to do owners and trainers used to advertise for staff in it.

Now, when I were born, me parents gave me biblical names, as was the wont at the turn of the century. Most kids born in the north got a name out of the bible. Well, my fayther went at it wholesale and gave me a right handle: Enoch Ebenezer Samson Noah William Birch. Well, a pal of mine were reading this paper one day in a pub and he says 'Eh, Willie, they're looking for folk like thee in t'Orient.' I took the paper off him and read the advert 'Enochs wanted for harem - must be good at massage'. Well, it were right up my street. So I catches a banana liner from Salford docks all the way to this potentate's country and when I gets to the front door of his palace I handed him my credentials. His servants carried me on a special mobile podium covered in ermine, made out of pure gold it were, and encrusted with jewels. It were proper sumptuous. I were given a feed of pig's eyes, olives and exotic spices from the markets of Baghdad, while scantily dressed maidens waited on me hand and foot. Funny, but it reminded me of me granny's in Oswaldtwistle a bit. She always made a fuss of me. Then, all of a sudden, the potentate yells 'Take your pants off, lad.' I thinks to messen, aye, aye, sod this for a game of sowjers! But seeing I were surrounded by big fellas, like Yorkshire forrards, with scimitars in their mitts, I had to do as I were told.

I realised that he were wanting to check me credentials, or lack of them, in my case. Now, when I looked at these big lackeys of his, I were sure one o' them were Jack Arkwright, and he gave me a wink. I'd rubbed big Jack down when I were on loan to Warrington. What the hell's he doing here, I thought? But it wasn't for me to reason why. So, I'm standing there with me kecks round me ankles, and up steps the potentate to do a check. When he sees me wedding tackle, he nearly has a fit! I suddenly realised as there'd been a printer's error in the paper. It should'a said eunuch of course. I tried to explain, but they don't parley lanky in t'Orient, so I gives the eye to the chap what faythers Jack Arkwright.

Now, this were a dangerous thing to do in the circumstances - you'd never know what he were thinking. Well, the big fella has a word with the potentate, who does a lot of humming and haaaing, until at last he says, 'I'll sue that bloody paper, and get me one and a tanner back. Thanks for translating owd lad.' Jack gave him an Uncle Joe's mint ball and all was well again.

I breathed a sigh of relief but I wasn't sure even then if one of those guards would turn Enoch here into a eunuch with one swipe of his blade. They were evil-looking swines and their scimitars were itching in their scabbards.

Well, I thanks big Jack Arkwright and buys him a gill in t'pub. I asked him how in heaven's name he knew the potentate. It seems when his nibs was a youngster, he'd been sent over to Saint 'Elens, Jack's home town, by his fayther, the Nawab of somewhere or other, to a finishing school to learn him how to talk english proper and that's where he met Jack. It were summer when I were there and Jack was over doing a bit of coaching..."

Willie's story was ended by the referee who appeared in the doorway.

"Two minutes lads," he announced.

The Bramfield players were laughing as Ossie Evans led them to the field. Mucker Casey, the big blind side-prop Rovers had bought from St. Helens Recreation, a breeding ground of big rough forwards, waited for his opposite number, Roughhouse Riley, to appear.

"Well, Mucker, shall we have it rough or smooth today?" asked Riley.

"Smooth, eh?" was the answer and the two props shook hands. They had played together for Wigan Highfield but there was no love lost on the field of battle.

"Think on, no rough stuff," said Riley as he walked away to join his team.

The game didn't start, it exploded. Mucker Casey caught the ball from the kick off and straight away Roughhouse Riley ran at him with his right knee up. Down went Mucker in agony as Ossie Evans ran over to complain to the ref. This was the cue for Ike Drinkwater, Rover's hooker, to clobber Riley, giving him a Wiggin butty right in the chops. Drinkwater was pulled away by Cowboy Smith while Roughhouse protested his innocence.

"It were this knee 'o mine ref, it twitches, I lost control of it. It's not my fault." This cut no notice with the official.

"I'm writing it down in book anyroad. What's your knee's name?" asked the man with the whistle.

Woodbine Willie was on the pitch dosing Mucker's groin with icy water from his magic sponge, while a tirade of boos was launched at the Bruddersby prop by the home crowd.

The incident set up an avalanche of catcalls and slow handclapping. For a few minutes, the poor referee was the most hated official in the world. The comments came thick and fast. What a game rugby league would be if referees were perfect! A sport for connoisseurs, but without fun. What would speccies do if they couldn't slag the ref? Rovers speccies were experts at baying at the referee: "*Get buggers on side*, ref," "*Wheer's your white stick, ref?*" "*Have you swallowed your pea, mister?*"

The latter was very popular comment from the boy's pen. "*He couldn't referee a bloody long-distance spitting match, yon mon. I reckon he's blind and dee-af.*" and "*Put him a Bruddersby jersey on! He's as biased as a set o' woods.*" And so on. The referee had heard it all before and simply waved the game on by giving a scrum.

Slipshod defending by the forwards saw the opposition pack charge through close to the try line. Poor tackling always incensed the Bramfield crowd. They could tolerate dropped

passes and faulty kicking, but not poor defence. Players who were 'nesh' were 'nowt a pound', as they said on the terrace.

"Get bloody stuck in, you big sod. Get his bloody legs, he's only a babby!"

It was an old woman, smothered in green and white woollies, who led the verbal assault on the Rovers pack. Not to be outdone, a wizened old man yelled *"Get 'em fettled! No wonder Bramfield's pack called t'easy six!"*

"Tackle him, not tickle him........ By the bloody heck, he couldn't tackle me grandad, yon mon,"

But when 'Roughhouse Riley' gave the Bramfield hooker a thump in the face the crowd's anger tuned on the opposition pack again. A section of the home speccies surged down the terrace and crashed through the flimsy, broken down fence. Policemen were specimens of manhood in those days. Two bobbies, who dwarfed even the tallest forward on the field, rushed to stop the crowds spilling onto the pitch. The incident was soon diffused, but the insult brigade were having a tea party.

"Bloody Norah! They'd get away with murder, this lot - get him off ref! Skennin' eck! He's dirtiest forrard in league, and ref turns a blind eye."

The referee was giving Riley a good old fashioned ticking off, but it was obvious he wasn't going to get an early bath.

"It's no use talking to yon mon, he's as thick as a Wigin butty," Bawled the old woman in the Rovers colours.

"Make a bloody example of him, ref, when he were born thi shudda kept the afterbirth and thrown babby away..." Even the referee laughed at that one.

"Go 'ome, ref! You're as useless as a one-legged man at an arse-kicking contest..." shouted the wizened old man.

"Boo... boo... boo... boo... boo... boo... boo... boo..." screamed the boys in the pen.

From the gas works end of the ground, across to the tripe works side of the embankment, across to the kids' best stand, the cat calls, jibes, boos and insults showered down on the offending forward and the referee like unrelenting hail. Joshua was furious, his face crimson with rage.

"I'm putting in a protest to Leeds, I am. Look, he's letting him stop on field, he should be suspended sine-die, should that lad. He's a bloody thug. Do they open prisons and let G.B.H. men out to play in your pack, Hadfield? Look at the ugly brute —— you can tell he's a bloody hoodlum. His face favvers King Kong's arse, and that's an insult to the gorilla."

Hadfield gave Joshua a painful dig in the ribs with his elbow. His false teeth rattled as he shouted angrily.

"Over reacting again, that's your trouble! You can't take it when one of your side gets a knock. It were nowt more than an over-enthusiastic shove. You're all soft in Lancasheer."

"Sod that for a game o' sowjers!" shouted the Rovers chairman, waving his arms around like an eccentric windmill and jumping up and down on the wooden floor of the stand. "Boo! boo! boo!" he screamed at the referee.

The Rovers were getting by far the worst of the hammer. Bruddersby Stanley were really playing well. Poor Cowboy Smith was having a nightmare of a game at stand-off. His first pass from the scrum-half had gone to ground and he had been tackled in possession four times on the run from the scrum. The Rovers three-quarters were starved of possession even though Ike Drinkwater, the hooker, was winning the scrums. Even Cowboy's defence was poor, he was a fish out of water as a half-back. His replacement at full-back was doing no better. After twenty minutes play he dropped a high ball under the posts and Stanley soon had another score when their right-winger intercepted and scored a glorious fifty yard try in the corner.

Joshua feared the worst. Defeat stared him in the face and when Stanley's full-back dropped a goal the game looked to be going down the slopstone for the Rovers. Yet like most diehards he was more inclined to blame the referee than the

Rovers players.

"Gerrum onside!" he roared as he bounced up and down on the planks.

"Go easy on them planks, Josh," advised Bert Kearsley, "tha's no lightweight, tha knows, we'll all end up on floor, and we'll have no money to spend on new welsh stand-off half. We'll have to repair stand."

Hadfield's ears twitched like sensitized antennae.

"Oh, so you're going after Powell, are you? You might be disappointed, gentlemen." He gave them a cold grin.

Joshua gave Bert a dirty look.

"Ee, I'm fair sorry, Joshua... it slipped out in excitement," mumbled an embarrassed Bert.

"Well, it's out in open now, Hadfield. I knew as thee are after him. Having been informed by one of your many spies about our activity. You'd stoop to anything. Yes, we are signing Powell, and it'll be in papers on Monday morning - so theer!"

The half-time whistle blew. Joshua blew a last raspberry at the referee before retiring to the pavilion with his two mates for a hot drink and to refill the club hot water bottle.

The second half was hardly any better for the Rovers, although Dodger Dean, the little winger, did score a fine try to make the score look more respectable. Cowboy moved back to full-back and Ossie Evans filled the stand-off berth, but it made no difference. Hadfield gloated out loud and Joshua cursed inwardly. In the battle of the roses Yorkshire had won the day to some pattern.

With Stanley leading by sixteen points to five Rovers speccies were leaving the ground in droves. Unknown to his co-directors Joshua had 'phoned Cardiff Rugby Union Club to see if Dai was there. By a stroke of good luck the game had been postponed and Joshua was told that Mr Powell was in the club house. Eventually they were connected and Joshua told the stand-off that his club had agreed to pay the fee. Powell was pleased but insisted that he must have proof before he told his club. He suggested that Joshua should tell the press who would then report it in the following Monday's papers.

"If I see it boyo, I'll come up, if not I'll be playing for Cardiff on Saturday at Blackheath, you'll have to come down to see me if you're still interested."

As the match drew to its conclusion, Joshua had gone to have a chat with the reporters in the press box at the top of the stand. Unknown to him an eavesdropper was noting his remarks. The snooper was none other than a Bruddersby director whom Joshua had never met. The reporters were delighted with the news and promised to get it hot-foot to the papers via the club pigeons, who were having a good feed of corn and water before their flight. When Hadfield was told the news by his eavesdropping director he smiled contentedly. He knew what action to take. If he had his way the news wouldn't reach the papers. Joshua was ever the gentleman and said cheerio to his rivals, even though he hated having to speak to them at all.

"Best team won." he admitted.

"Aye, and you'll be sick of us Joshua," said Hadfield, "drawn against us in t' cup and all, then your 'A' team has to come to our ground, we haven't lost a second team game this season. It's our season is this."

"We'll see about that, Hadfield," Josh muttered as he headed for the pavilion and the consolation of a glass of brandy.

Hadfield Barnacre's chauffeur saluted when his employer arrived back at the limousine after the match. He was surprised to see him back so early. As a rule he went into the club-house for a drink after a game. This time Hadfield had other ideas. He pointed to waste land which lay across the road. "Drive over there and park." he commanded.

Hadfield was a crack shot both with air guns and double barrelled rifles and had represented Yorkshire on a number of occasions. As luck would have it his air gun was in his car boot. The spectators had almost left the area and a quietness had descended, aided and abetted by the eeriness of the late afternoon air, when a flurry of wings overhead told Hadfield that it was time for business. With deadly aim he shot the four pigeons, one after the other. A cold blooded and precise execution.

"That'll make owd Joshua get a flaming telephone!" he whispered as he replaced the gun in the boot of the car.

"You may drive back to Bruddersby now, Jackson."

Hadfield Barnacre shot the Rover's pigeons down with cold blooded precision

Chapter Four

Joshua turns the tables on Hadfield

It was the Monday morning after the defeat at the hands of Bruddersby Stanley. Joshua had spent a rather fitful night tossing and turning and Phoebe Maude had got up to make a cup of tea.

"I sometimes wish I'd wed a man who had no interest in sport," she muttered, but she didn't really mean it. She knew rugby league was her husband's life but she would have been more content if he didn't worry about it so much. Joshua was an anxious being, she knew that only too well. It was this business of the welsh stand-off half; he couldn't wait to read the papers. He was convinced the northern dailies would give the story a good spread. It was no use, neither of them could sleep properly, so by the time the papers arrived they had eaten their breakfasts.

Joshua had ordered three different papers. The distinctive sound of newspapers falling on to linoleum alerted them to the fact that they had arrived. Phoebe Maude dashed to pick them up and took them to her husband who was sitting in the armchair by the open fire. He tried the *Daily Dispatch* first — — no news. Mystified, he rummaged through the pages of the *Daily Mail* but no joy there either. He couldn't believe it, surely the *Daily Herald* would mention it? It was a deflated and disappointed chairman who finally flung the papers across the room in his frustration. "What the hell's gone wrong lass?

They're always dead keen to get rugby league news in the papers."

"'Appen you ought to get a telephone installed Joshua?"

"Nay, lass, pigeons never let us down."

At that moment there was a knock on the door. Joshua opened it to find a gangling lad of about ten years of age, with a flat cap and a runny nose.

"Me mam told me to come here before I went to school. It's about pigeons, mister."

"What about 'em?"

"I found three on a field on Sat'day. They were dead. Me dad reckons as they'd been shot by an airgun or summat."

"Have you got bodies lad?"

"Oh no mister, we've etten 'em for us tea. Me mam made pigeon pie. It were good an all —— but I've got these."

He handed Joshua three small lead name plates. All three bore the inscription: *Bramfield R.L. Club Express Results Service.*

Joshua went to the mill 'early doors' to attend to urgent business. He wanted to get it finished before he visited Stanley Keighley, the chief scout for the club. Joshua made his living out of the cotton mill but a lot of his time was spent on rugby business. As the chairman he never knew the second he would be dashing off signing players and attending to all manner of things appertaining to the smooth running of a club. They had kept a secretary at one time but during the club's doldrums days he had been paid off. With the aid of his co-directors, the Kearsley brothers, Joshua somehow muddled through, but the anxiety of it all played havoc with his waterworks. To put it bluntly, he couldn't stop peeing. Nothing could be done, the doctors said. It was due to worry. Give up the chairmanship of the Rovers and rest, they advised. They might as well have asked a seagull not to crap on the recumbent bathers at Blackpool during Wakes Week. Rugby league was his life and Joshua *was* rugby league, *THE VERY ESSENCE* of it, one of the best ambassadors the game had ever had. He was his own man and it must be stated that he did things in his own inimitable style.

The business took longer than expected but at last, at eleven o'clock, he left the mill to call on Stanley Keighley. His mind was once more focusing on the plight of the club. They had played eleven games in the league and won seven, not a bad start, but when it is explained that they had lost the last three on the run it will be easier to understand Joshua's concern. The rot had suddenly set in.

It was a bitter cold day as he set off from the mill in his heavy crombie overcoat and hard bowler hat, an imposing figure, all eighteen stones of him. The chairman was well known to all and sundry, rich and poor in Bramfield. He was an approachable man, a working class lad who had risen to the dizzy heights of mill owner. If ever a man had struggled against difficulties and succeeded it was 'Jovial Josh', as he was affectionately known in the town. He had known the pangs of hunger as a child when the town was held in the grip of abject poverty; his parents had scraped and sifted for coal on the slag heaps and had been very familiar with soup kitchens and charity hand-outs. Joshua made no secret of the fact that as a child he was clothed by courtesy of the local Clog and Stocking fund, a charity which did wonderful work in northern towns. He was a man of the people.

As he crossed the ancient bridge over the canal he caught a whiff of the gas works, its putrid stench blending in an odious cocktail with the outpouring of filth from the chemical plant.

The stink from the abattoir didn't help, it turned his stomach over and when a gust of wind suddenly blew the unsavoury aroma of boiled vinegar from the pickle factory in his face he almost vomited. The canal depressed him even more. It was full of old prams and dead cats. Joshua smiled to himself when he thought how the canal could take on romantic qualities in the moonlight. If you had a good imagination the lamp of the moon could turn even a putrid canal into a silver lagoon. His walk took him down a dirty snicket known as 'Moggie's Entry'. At the end of this foul thoroughfare there was a wonderful view of Bramfield. Wonderful, that is if the viewer was not expecting to see a land of milk and honey. For this was a dirty industrial town, but judged in that light it was a classic example of what havoc necessary industry can wreak on a once beautiful landscape. Set in a vale of the Pennines, it nestled below a permanent pall of dirty smoke from the factories. Very rarely were the hills visible, the folk were trapped by the noxious end products of the places that provided them with a living. Only at Wakes Week, the annual holiday, would the surrounding countryside come into view. With the factories shut and the tall smoke stacks redundant for a week the smoke would clear. It was almost magical. This in itself was a tonic, and a wonderful bonus for those people who couldn't get away to Blackpool or Southport or go hiking in the Lake District. They were suddenly aware that they lived in a town surrounded by hills where vegetation actually existed and flourished. A dear old dirty town, but Joshua loved it and the folk who lived in it.

Slowly he picked his way carefully across waste land full of pot holes and rubbish. At the end of the field there was a flight of cobbled steps that took you into the high street. It was hard work for a chap of Joshua's stature; what's more, there was no where to have a pee. So it was with some relief that he came to a wall behind which he urinated, keeping a weather eye out for anyone approaching. Even a man of his standing would be run in by the local bobby for committing a nuisance. As he fastened his flies he thought about the wall and all it stood for in the town. On the other side of it unemployed men had stood for generations, a meeting place for depressed and desperate men vainly hoping that a factory would seek them out.

Joshua could never forget the looks of abject despair on the faces of these men. Times had improved, there was no doubt about that, but prosperity did not know the town of Bramfield. Most folk simply existed and were glad of it. His mind went back to the time two years before when the town council had turned its back on the club. Only by sheer hard work and a near miracle had the Rovers survived. What a disaster it would have been for the town had the club folded. Joshua would never forget those evil days when the stygian blackness of financial doom was at his throat. He had sworn that they would never return.

He was negotiating a steep cobbled 'brew' made treacherou by a hard frost when he heard a familiar voice greet him.

"Good morning to thee, master Joshua lad," It was old Molly Flanagan. Her clog irons were sparking on the frosty cobble setts and her shawl was pulled tight around her frail, spindly body in a futile attempt to keep the intense cold at bay.

"By gum, lad it's cowd. 'Am frozzen."

"It's coming from Siberia, Molly," said Joshua.

"Nay, it's worse than that, it's coming from Owdam, Watersheddings way. It's coldest spot in creation is that. It's a good job it's not a Yorksheer wind, they'd charge for it, them tight fisted tykes."

Joshua laughed heartily. Bramfield was very close to Yorkshire and the townsfolk always emphasised their Lancashire roots by making derogatory remarks about the white rose county. Joshua dug deeply into his overcoat pocket for a silver three penny piece which he gave to the old woman.

"Ee, God bless thee, Mr Hepplethwaite lad. I'll treat mesen to a bag o' tripe bits and a cup of hot Bovril in t'market hall." Joshua shook hands and wished her well. He had only progressed a few yards when she called to him. "By the way, when are you getting a decent out-half, Mr Hepplethwaite?"

Joshua chuckled to himself. Even old Molly was concerned. Something had to be done.

"Oh, bloody Flaming Norah! It's Sam Crabwater." Joshua muttered to himself, but alas, there was no escape. Old Crabwater the plumber was bearing down upon him. Sam was a moaner. There was always something wrong.

"I want a word with thee, Chairman Hepplethwaite,"

"What about, Sam lad?"

"I've done drains up at t'club. What a bloody job! I've added seven and sixpence to the bill. I had to get long rods out, took me all day. Bloody disgrace it were."

"I did tell you they were badly blocked Sam,"

"Blocked? You couldn't have done better with cement. You know what's wrong, don't you? Why, you've only got two inch pipes but someone's got a three inch arse hole —— I'm putting seven and sixpence on t'bill."

"Reet, Sam lad, send it to the club. It'll be paid, never fear."

Joshua brushed past the plumber, ignoring a tirade of criticisms and comments about the drainage system at the ground. He headed across the railway bridge but he couldn't have chosen a worse time. Filthy, vile smoke from an engine passing below engulfed him like a black shroud. A blanket of soot covered his face and his eyes felt as if they were on fire. He gave an involuntary gulp and out fell his bottom teeth. For at least a minute Joshua couldn't see. At last, with the help of a handkerchief, he made out the last of a whole string of coal wagons disappearing into the gloom towards Yorkshire. His teeth were nowhere to be found. The spaces between the wooden planks of the bridge told him the worst.

"Bloody hell! Things are getting wuss". He muttered. A young telegraph lad from the post office was wheeling his bicycle across the bridge. Joshua asked him to see if he could find the teeth on the lines. The lad scrambled down the embankment but there was no sign of them. Joshua forked out another tanner.

"Thanks lad. I'll go to the station. I need a slash in lavvy anyway. Is me face dirty?"

"Dirty? I thought thee were a black man at first, mister."

The Station Master promised to find the coal train's destination. Joshua was on a very short fuse and the grin on the official's face didn't help. He obviously thought it was a great joke.

"I'll ring thee at Mr Keighley's undertaking parlour if I hear owt," he said, still grinning.

Having to go to the station had put quite a distance on his walk to the Keighley's residence at Arkwright Sidings. Josh asked the Station Master if could he nip across the line and up the bank. He knew this led to a disused coal tip from where he could go up a ginnell which led to the foot of Stanley's street. His mind was focused on the business ahead and he had forgotten that it was Monday. Without thinking he walked into a clothes line full of washing. The rope took his hat of with the skill of a guillotine and at the same time a wet sheet enveloped him like a shroud. As he struggled and fought a losing battle with the clinging sheet he brought down the pole. A pile of washing fell into the mud.

"What the bloody hell is going on?"

His blood froze. He recognised Ada Mudge's voice. Ada was a spinster of some notoriety. Fourteen stones if she was an ounce, built like a second-row-forward.

"You bloody gormless puddin!" she roared. "Have you nowt between your ears?"

Joshua peeled the wet sheet from his face and saw Ada's formidable form bearing down on him with a rolling pin in her hand. In such a mood Ada would have put the entire Wigan pack to flight. She raised the rolling pin above her head, for all the world like a marauding dervish.

"It were an accident, lass, I'm sorry," he pleaded.

"Sorry! Accident! What the hell are you doing up a back ginnell on a wash day, any road. Oh, it's you is it? —— Hepplethwaite the councillor?"

"I'm not on council now, Ada lass,"

"You're no use nor ornament. Any road — you're supposed to look after folks' interests on t'council, not ruin their Monday wash. I want compensating for this, do you hear, Mr Councillor?"

Joshua dug deeply into his crombie.

"Here's half a crown lass, and I can't tell thee how sorry I am, I've got a lot on my mind."

Ada Mudge would have put the entire Wigan pack to flight.

Ada took the coin and marched off. As he wearily trudged the remaining hundred yards to his destination he cursed his luck. Everyone in the north knew Monday was wash-day. Never go down a ginnell on a Monday morning, was an unwritten rule. Fancy getting a face full of wet washing. He was furious with himself. To make matters worse his wife would get to know. Ada had a mouth as wide as the canal and his encounter with her underwear would be all over the town. He cursed his stupidity. There was so much on his mind, that was the trouble. Folks think being a club chairman is a cushy job, he mused. They've no ruddy idea! How wrong can they be? If things are going badly they're baying for your blood saying you couldn't organise a what-not in a brewery. His co-directors were great hearted lads but as chairman he had to carry the can. If he could only land a top class out-half he'd be the happiest man in the world. 'Appen things would improve, aye 'appen ... or 'appen not.

As Joshua was making heavy weather of his visit to their terraced house in Arkwright Sidings, the Keighley's were having their dinner. Monday dinner was always 'early doors', for Clara Keighley had been hard at work since seven o'clock

Clara Keighley loved a good Monday washday.

doing the weekly wash. She loved a good wash did Clara, and often spoke eloquently on the blessing of a good drying wind, in the same way that a student of literature waxes enthusiasticly upon the works of a favourite playwright or poet.

She loved the ritual of doing exactly what her mother and grandmother had done before her. The water was taken from the tap in the back yard and heated in the copper boiler.

This was carried in a pail to the great iron tub where the clothes were pummelled and poked with a three legged wooden contraption known as a dolly peg. Stanley had promised to buy her a gas boiler but had never got round to it, but Clara never complained. She was at her happiest when she was working. Like most northern women she was used to hard work. There was dignity in it and you just got on with it. Her friends couldn't understand her still having gaslight in the house, a large portion of the town had electricity. With her Stanley being an undertaker, she was considered to be middle class. But Clara didn't trust electricity. It wasn't safe she claimed, and what's more she never wanted to give the impression that she was 'owt more than she was' — she was born a working lass and she wanted to remain so. Clara was enjoying her dinner. It was her favourite.

"Ee, by gum, there' nowt so tasty as trotters and onions, Stanley. I love to dip bread in the juice," she said to her husband.

"It's good grub, Clara lass," agreed Stanley, belching loudly.

"Are you worried over t'club, lad?" asked his wife grimly.

"I am an all, lass, three defeats on trot and playing away next week at Liverpool. They're doing well. It's a funny ground is that, surrounded by a dog-track. Nobody likes playing there, it's not like playing on a proper rugby pitch."

"Well, I hope you sign that welsh lad, Stanley. It'll be a feather in your cap for it was you what spotted him first. Mr Hepplethwaite should be grateful he's got such a good scout. I wonder why he was off-handed when you saw him at the match on Saturday?"

"I think he blames me for summat, he said he were coming round today. Me and him are going off to London on Friday to watch the new lad play against Blackheath, you know that lass, don't you?"

"Aye, and think on, no shinaniking, and keep away from strong waters, they don't suit you. Many a marriage has been wrecked on the rocks of drunkenness and debauchery, think on. The vicar were only on about it last week at the Women's League of Temperance. He reckons pubs are evil places, does vicar."

"You were in one yourself last week at supporters' club do."

"Appen I were, but it was in t'room above pub. That doesn't count. And further more, although I helped get the hot pot ready, I refused to help with the trifle."

"What did you do that for lass?"

"Because there were sherry in it. I don't approve of owt alcoholic."

She pointed to a framed tract on the wall above the harmonium. It read: '*Look not upon the wine when it is red, for it will stingeth like a serpent and biteth like an adder*'.

"Stick by that lad, and you can't go far wrong. And talking about the hot pot do, I didn't approve of that joke Albert Heneberry made about thawing hard grounds before matches."

"Oh, you mean the one about the brassieres instead of Braziers?"

"Don't defile this house, Stanley Keighley! Don't mention them words here. Think on, it's devil's talk."

"What's wrong woman, don't you wear 'em yourself? Brassieres I mean."

"That's as mebbe, but you aren't supposed to know that. Them's delicate matters and not for likes o'thee."

"You should have been a nun lass."

"I'm just a simple lass what stands up for decency. You laughed at Albert's joke. Encouraging him, that's what you do when you laugh. He's too fond of mucky talk is that lad."

Stanley groaned inwardly. He was going to get a lecture, he could feel it in his water. Once Clara got on the subject of 'being pure in all things' he could be there for a couple of hours. She fancied herself as a lay preacher did Clara, but she hadn't the nerve to do it in a church or out in the street. Stanley was a captive audience. Any road, he'd be off to London with Mr Hepplethwaite soon and he could have a few pints of ale and a laugh.

It was a glum life when he thought about it, being an undertaker and wed to Clara. She was just getting into full flow, despite tucking into 'spotted dick', when there was a knock on the front door. Stanley peeped through the curtains and was glad to see the portly figure of the club chairman. He didn't like the look on his face though. Summat was up. He could always tell when Joshua was in a bad mood.

"It's Mr Hepplethwaite, Clara,"

"Hang on, don't open door. I'll just dust aspidistra."

She placed a mob cap on her head, which was full of curlers, and set about the plant with a feather duster. Joshua had to knock again. This time Stanley opened it and feigned surprise.

"Ee, by the heck, fancy it being thee, Mr Hepplethwaite. Come in and put thee feet on t'mantle piece and spit in t' fire — tha's reet welcome, me owd jockey."

"Thank you Stanley. Good day to you, Clara, lass. It's a cold wind. It'll freeze washing 'appen. I didn't think to chuck me cap in."

"You don't need to do that here lad, Mr Hepplethwaite. Will you take a cup o' tea? We're just finishing us 'spotted dick'. You look fair clemmed. It's winter now and no mistake. It's hot brick weather, but then you'll have one o' them posh hot water bottles. 'Appen a rubber one 'an all?"

"Nay lass. A hot brick has always done me and Phoebe Maude. It heats a bed up better than all the modern inventions, does a good brick. I'm sorry to call on wash day lass but I've got something very important to discuss with Stanley. Can I take me coat off, lass?"

The chairman peeled off his heavy coat and handed it to Stanley. Clara was pouring the chairman a cup of tea when she suddenly froze and pointed to the floor. "And what might that be?" she trumpeted.

A pair of knickers had fallen from the coat.

"Er — 'appen — er — well —— er, I think they must belong to Ada Mudge up street --— aye —— 'appen so --— . I'll return 'em on my way home."

He tried to kick them out of sight with his foot. Clara gave a sanctimonious screech.

"So you admit it do you? Coming here to my house knowing I'm church, and you a married man. You should be ashamed of yourself!"

Joshua tried to laugh it off but Clara only let out another screech.

"Nay, lass, it's not what you think --- it was like this see --- I can explain it all ---"

"No explanation in the world will do. You come in here with Ada Mudge's underwear in your greatcoat pocket. I'll not take tea with fornicators and adulterers what consort with profligate women and strumpets."

Joshua rose to his full height. "Now look here Clara, I don't like your insinuations one little bit. I bumped into Miss Mudge's washing line when I walked up the snicket and one of the articles must have fallen into me pocket. Surely you know me better than that, Clara? Why, if Salome herself danced in your parlour I wouldn't give her a look. I've too much on me mind lass for wenching."

"Salome?" asked Stanley "Wasn't she the wench what danced naked in front of Harrods?"

"Herod, you crate egg!" bawled Clara. "You never did go to Sunday school, did you? Too busy playing the devil's games like billiards and shove halfpenny. There's no religion in you at all."

"You've enough for two of us, lass," said her husband.

"Aye, Stanley's reet, Clara. Being religious doesn't mean seeing bad in everybody else. It means being charitable, seeing two sides of everything, giving the benefit of the doubt. Too quick to judge, Clara lass, that's you. What I've told you is the truth. Miss Mudge gave me a mouthful 'an all. I gave her half a crown for her troubles —."

"Oh, so you did, did you?" retorted Clara.

"For another wash, lass! Compensation, it's you what's got a mucky mind. Do you think for one minute if I wanted to indulge in clandestine affairs I'd pick Ada Mudge? She's not the epitome of nubile maidenhood, is she?"

"You've taken the very words out of me mouth, Mr Hepplethwaite," said Stanley.

"I believe you, I mean to say, that Ada has taken her pitcher to the well a few times; she's no chicken,"

"More like a bloody old boiler, if you ask me. You should have heard the mouthful she came out with, Stanley."

"No swearing here, Mr Hepplethwaite, think on!"

"Sorry, Clara lass,"

Joshua sat at the table, glad to be near the fire. "I've lost me bottom teeth lass, I'll have to sup tea out of a saucer."

"What's happened to thee teeth?" asked Stanley.

"They fell in a coal wagon. Enough of my problems. Pour us another saucer full lass, last one's gone cowd with all thee blabbin'."

Clara gave Stanley a funny look which translated meant that Mr Hepplethwaite was going off his head. Joshua took a long pull at the hot tea, wiped his lips with a red spotted handkerchief, and looked Stanley straight in the eye.

"I've got a bone to pick with thee, lad. It's not a chicken bone either, more like a dinosaur."

Clara's face lit up. "Isn't that one o' them pre-hysterical animals? We learned about them at school. I had a picture of one of them other ones, a Brontysorearse, they called it. I loved that story of Conan Doyle's an' all. *The Lost World* it were called. They find a place where all these creatures still exist. It were me favourite subject at school. They had reet funny names. I believe in Loch Ness Monster, I do, it's a throwback to all them millions of years ago, is that lad. Do you believe in it Mr Hepplethwaite?"

"I've got an open mind Clara. The only monster I believe in is Hadfield Barnacre."

"Ee, they did give me some fun at school, did them monsters,"

Joshua was growing impatient, Clara got on his nerves very quickly. He could only take so much of the lass. Stanley could see the agitation on the chairman's face.

"Shut thee cake 'ole, Clara lass," he shouted, "chairman's not come here to listen to thee. Tha's got too much o'what cat licks its bottom wi'. Now what do you want to say to me, Mr Chairman?" said Stanley, refilling Joshua's saucer with tea.

"Did you bury Mary Alice Postlethwaite?"

"'Appen ...? I may have done. Is she dead?"

"Course she's ruddy dead! Though knowing thee, it wouldn't surprise me if you buried live ones."

"Hang on, I were getting mixed up with Mary Alice Thistlethwaite," said Stanley.

"Poslethwaite's the name Stanley, not Thistlethwaite," Joshua was being very deliberate, "have you got cloth ears?"

"Well, what of it? What if I did commit her to the earth, I am an undertaker?" retorted the aggrieved scout.

"Because Mary Alice was the cousin of Hadfield Hardacre who is related by marriage to Jeremiah Crumpsall. Crumpsall was Mary Alice's second cousin twice removed."

"Nay, first cousin Mr Hepplethwaite," interjected Clara. "It were Matilda Jane Postlethwaite what were his second cousin, she were Mary Alice's step sister." she informed them.

"Nay she weren't," said Stanley. "Matilda Jane were no relation to the Crumpsalls. She wed a plumber from Mumps, he had piles bad."

Clara was adamant. "Nay Stanley —— you're wrong lad. It were bad breath. He had to have it removed. It was your uncle Fred's lodger what had piles, he were from Mumps — they were galloping piles an' all."

"Nay lass, I tell thee as —"

Joshua once again rose to his full height. He towered above the Keighleys as he roared "I've come here to talk about rugby league. I don't care if Mary Alice married the king of China. Now let's get on with the matter in hand!"

"Will thee tell us what's up then?" said Stanley.

"My bet is that Crumpsall arranged the funeral and he asked you to do it."

"What of it?" said Stanley.

"Well, he gets the sherry out doesn't he? Are you with me?" The chairman's words were heavily laden with sarcasm.

"Well — he were hospitable when I went to his house. Yes, I had a couple. I were only being courteous —"

"And you told him we were after Dai Powell, I suppose —" said Josh fiercely.

"Well — 'appen — but it were confidential like,"

"Confidential me backside. Sorry Clara lass, but your husband would make a saint swear. You knew that he was related to Barnacre and still you told him?"

"Well, I forgot that. I'm sorry if I've done summat wrong, Mr chairman, but he's not interested in rugby league since his wife ran off with that scrum-half from Salford."

"Nay, he might not be interested in the sport Stanley. What he does like is getting his own back on me and t'Rovers. You know the flaming row we had when him and t'council refused to help the club when we were skint. He hates me, does Crumpsall."

"How do we stand now then?" asked Stanley. Joshua had decided to keep the incident of the pigeons to himself for the moment. He knew his scout couldn't keep his trap shut when he'd had a few gills. The story would be all over the town and Joshua would be the laughing stock. It was going to be bad enough over Ada Mudge's knickers without anything else.

"I were all for offering Powell more money to persuade him to make up his mind pronto, but it's all gone wrong. So we're definitely going to London. Powell's team, Cardiff, are playing Blackheath, as you know, so it'll be ideal way of meeting lad and trying to get him to the dotted line before Hardacre gets to him — that's if he hasn't already, of course."

At this juncture the telephone rang. Clara was afraid of 'them new fangled gadgets' as she called telephones, and waved Stanley to answer it.

"Be sharp lad! I can't stand that noise!"

"It's for you, Mr Hepplethwaite, it's railway station." said Stanley.

Joshua took the mouthpiece up eagerly. "Hepplethwaite here— you what? Well, of all t'places to fetch up at! Well, thanks any road. I'll pick 'em up later today — good day to you."

"Good news Mr Chairman?" asked the scout.

"Aye, they've found me teeth. They ended up in a siding in Bruddersby, of all t'places. They've put 'em on a passenger train. It's been a hard day, Stanley lad, one thing after another. Let's hope the week gets better, it can't get wuss — can we have some more tea, lass?"

"I'll put kettle on t' hob," said Clara, "but now it's my turn to speak me mind to me husband. You might think that I'm a crank, but I do love the Rovers. I'll never forgive thee Stanley if Bruddersby get Powell. You've let side down. Traitor in 'camp, that's you, and all because of booze! All my married life your weakness for spirituous ales has dogged me. You're noted for it lad and I'm ashamed of thee! What would vicar say? I mean, he's a supporter an' all, tha knows. He has a season ticket has t'vicar. Think on, if Powell signs for Bruddersby I'll never open me mouth to thee again! Now, if only to show how much I love the Rovers I'm going to give a donation. It's towards fee for t'new union lad, if you get him." Clara knelt down by the fire place. "Turn thee back, Stanley!" she ordered.

"Why lass?"

"Cos I said so! Shift thee sen."

When she was convinced that her husband's back was turned Clara lifted a tile from the floor of the fire place and took out a ten shilling note.

"That's a gradely gesture, Clara.," said the chairman, pocketing the note.

"It's not for ale, think on," she reminded him, wagging a finger.

"I suppose club will be near skint if you do get him?" she asked.

"Our bank balance will be very depleted lass, that's a fact." admitted Joshua.

"If only there was some local chap with lots of brass to hand out. A philatelist I mean," commented Clara.

"Aye, it would be lovely, Clara, but we live in the real world and Rovers never meet them sort. It's all uphill with our club. Still, we're doing O.K. and perhaps we'll see the great days return. 'Appen you'll be gettin' a new dress for Wembley, lass."

"Ee, what a nice thought. You'll look after my husband, won't you, Mr Hepplethwaite? It's a city of sin is London.

I don't want him going off with one o' them destitutes, and keep out o' them nude clubs what you hear about. Vicar says they're evil places —"

"How does he know - has he been in one?", goaded her husband. Joshua patted her on the shoulder to reassure her.

"I promise he'll come to no harm — well, I'm off now. Oh, I almost forgot Ada's unmentionables, I'll put 'em through her front door. I don't want another mouthfull. I bet her teeth's glad when she's asleep, she'd talk hind leg off a donkey, would that lass."

Stanley went to the front step to see the chairman off. "Are you putting a ten shilling note in Ada's smalls?". There was a smirk on his face. Joshua was not amused at Stanley's smutty remark.

"I don't think that's funny, Stanley. I've a good mind to give thee the sack for that. You'd better watch thee sen lad or you'll be out of club on thee ear. Think on — oh, and by the way, train's at seven thirty on Friday morning. So be theer and keep theeself sober! Are you with me? Think on!"

Chapter Five

Two Lanky Lads in London

The train journey from Bramfield to London had been an uneventful one for Stanley and Joshua. They were now walking up and down the platform at Paddington trying to keep warm by waving their arms about like two overweight penguins.

"I'm glad the thaw's set in, although it sucks the blood out of you," said Joshua, his false teeth chattering, and his chilblains smarting. "I'm reet glad the Blackheath game's going ahead. We want to get this business sorted. When you rang Blackheath to see if the ground were O.K., did you disguise your voice?" asked Stanley of his chairman.

"Did I 'ell as like," snorted Joshua indignantly. "I'm a Lancashire lad and proud of it. Why should I disguise me voice? I'm not a ruddy spy."

Stanley explained his question to Joshua. "Being a scout like me you get used to using subterfuge. They hate our guts in this part of the world. They think t'north's inhabited by wild beasts." Joshua nodded. "They're thinking of Widnes forrards, but I get your drift Stanley. The bloke who answered the 'phone sounded proper lardy-dah. When I went to sleep last night I had visions of him dressed up like a village squire with a riding crop in his hand and a bottle of Dows port in the other; and him chasing me out of a posh club house as he yelled obscenities at me. When we go t'match tomorrow we mustn't stand together; they won't know me, but you being a scout and having travelled around, you'd better wear a disguise. I've got one in my case in 'digs'. It's what's known as a false hirsute appendage in espionage circles; in other words a beard."

"Don't thee worry Mr Hepplethwaite, I'll wear it. I'm not a proud man. I'll never forget that time I went to watch a forrard at Old Etonians. I were spotted by a chap in t'bar, a brigadier he were. Proper toffee-nosed he were, He must have been an expert in accents because he called me a northern snooper and set his beagles on me. I ran like hell out of the club house and across the field. Lucky I had a steak puddin' on me. I threw it to the dogs and they stopped to eat it, which gave me enough time to get through a hole in the fence and on to a bus what was passing."

"Appen we'd better get a couple of steak puddins' then. By gum, it's cowd, Stanley. Let's have a cup from t'flask. I could drink hot tea till cows come wom. It's colder than sitting in Rochdale's best stand, is this station. It plays up me 'water works' does the cold. That's the only snag with rugby league. It's always cold. Best time is September when I can get a bit of blackberrying in. Nice warm sun burning down on as you wander down country lanes and along bank of t'river in Trough of Bowland, or 'appen Whalley - - - - you can't lick it Stanley. The south's alreet but there's too many southerners in it. If we could somehow get shut of southerners, exile 'em to Isle of Man, then fill t'south with overflow from t'north, we could have rugby league nationally, not to mention long distance spitting and crown green bowling."

"I agree Mr Hepplethwaite... I do 'an all. We could have black puddin' contests with grand final at Wembley, fried bread throwing, and 'how long can you keep a ferret down your trousers?' I could do with southerners if only they'd speak proper. Someone ought to learn 'em."

Stanley could normally go for hours without visiting the W.C., even when he'd had a skin full of beer. But for once he was in urgent need of a convenience.

"I'm fair brastin' for a slash!" he exclaimed before dashing off down the platform.

This meant that Joshua was left on his own. Anyone observing the scene would have commented on how happy the Bramfield chairman looked as he sat on a milk churn sipping hot tea from his flask. They could not have known that those mischievous gremlins of fate who had plagued him all week had not finished their impish work. In fact, their armoury of knavery was far from exhausted. A train was pulling into the platform as Joshua chewed one of Phoebe Maude's cheese and chutney sandwiches as an announcement came over the loudspeaker.

"The train now arriving at platform six is the 8 o'clock from Plymouth - - - - Plymouth train!"

When the train pulled up out stepped a young lady, aristocratic and demure, dressed rather inappropriately in attire more suited to warmer climes. On her head was perched a large picture hat and in her arms she clutched a Pekinese. She looked for all the world as if she had stepped out of one of Mr C. B. Cochran's famous revues. She was obviously distressed.

She tottered across on high heels, heading straight for Joshua.

"Oh, do be a darling - - - - do tell me where one can relieve oneself. The Southern line will insist on carriages without corridors. One gets rather desperate when travelling, does one not?"

Joshua pointed with a thumb up the platform.

"Have you bin taken short lass? It's up top end. I'm troubled with me sphincter mesen."

"Oh you are a pet - - - - hold Snoopy Sam for me will you, there's a darling. I won't be long."

If there was one thing Joshua really hated it was Pekinese dogs. Whippets and Jack Russells he could cope with, but not fiddly arsed tackle like Pekinese. He'd sooner have nursed a ferret. They say dogs can tell when they are not liked. Snoopy Sam certainly could. It gave Joshua's right hand a nip with its needle-like teeth.

"Get down you bloody little sod!" yelled the Rovers man who dropped the dog on the floor, whereupon it deposited an obnoxious object upon the platform.

"Oh, bloody hell, dog shit! That's all we want." he groaned. Once again he felt the cruel hand of fate upon him. He toyed with the idea of easing it over the side of the platform with his foot, but the passengers in the train were watching. The incident had not missed the deadly eye of the Station Master who promptly headed straight for Joshua.

Wearing a top hat and clad in a gold embellished uniform, complete with cane, he was the epitome of bumptious autocracy. In the north he would have been called a 'bloody twerp'. He was the boss of the station and everybody knew it. Joshua was at his wits' end to know what to do, but then he had a brain wave. He covered the obnoxious mound with his bowler

hat and started to whistle nonchalantly *'Yes, we have no bananas!'* But it was to no avail. The little poochs' egregious act had landed him in 'Dicky's Meadow', as they say in Bolton. The station gubernator was red in the face and pointed at Joshua's hard hat with his cane of office.

"I know what you are hiding and I won't have it!" he bellowed.

"Very well then, share it out among the porters," replied Joshua.

"That is my office," the official pointed to a glass window high above the platform, "I will expect you there in one minute. This incident will be reported and I intend to make an example of you. Do not delay!" Joshua blew a raspberry.

"I don't like your tone young man. You've got ideas above your station - - - - - ee - - - - - ee - - - - - that were a good one! - - - No sense of humour you southerners. They even think Max Miller's funny. He's not a patch on Frank Randle!"

By this time Stanley had arrived back on the platform.

"What's up Mr Hepplethwaite? Do you want me to sort him out? 'Appen a knuckle butty?"

The pompous official was livid with rage. He whirled his cane above his head. "Ugh! I can see you are nothing but a couple of ignorant savages from Yorkshire!"

"Bloody insult!" yelled Joshua, "we're Lancashire born and bred. Calling us tykes indeed! Let's send lads round to duff him up, Stanley."

The Station Master decided to drop the charges for safety's sake and disappeared up the stairs with the speed and agility of an Olympic hurdler. Alan Edwards, the Salford flier, couldn't have made a speedier getaway.

"The train approaching platform five is the nine o'clock from Cardiff," sang out the platform announcer.

"Come on Stanley, I reckon that's the train we want. Our lad should be on it —— let's be dooi'n."

A blanket of black oily smoke enveloped the entire station

concourse as the approaching train pulled up with screeching brakes at platform five. The people leaving the train were undistinguished grey spectres in an eerie fog, until at last they took on human shape.

"There he is!" said Stanley, pointing excitedly. "I'd tell him in two million. You can see from the t'way he walks he's an athlete."

A young man of middle height approached them. From broad muscular shoulders his body tapered down through a slim wiry figure to small, almost dainty feet. At first sight he could have been taken for a ballet dancer, but on close observation there was a ruggedness about the face which told that he was a man used to physical contact.

The Rovers scout greeted him like an old friend. "Are yer all reet, Dai owd lad?"

"Stanley boyo! how are you? It's good to see you, Stanley bach."

They shook hands warmly. The voice was baritonial, rich and undulating; in layman's terms 'sing song'. There was a warmth and friendliness about him which immediately impressed Joshua. Stanley introduced his chairman to the rugby union man.

"Meet Mr Hepplethwaite, chairman of the Rovers."

"Ow do," said Joshua shaking hands with the stand-off,

"It's grand to meet thee lad, I could tell you were a player by just watching you walk along the platform. Some blokes have an eye for a whippet or a ferret, or 'appen a comely wench, but I've got an eye for a footballer. I reckon you'll strip big too."

Stanley cast a critical eye in favour of the union man. "Five foot eight and eleven stones nine pounds, give or take an ounce,"

"Spot on Stanley boyo! Are you a P.T. instructor as well as a scout? You've got an expert eye."

"He's an undertaker," said Joshua, bringing the enthusiastic scout back to reality. Dai Powell looked a shade embarrassed.

"We'll discuss it over a drink, lad," said Joshua, ever the

diplomat.

"I need warming up. There's no colder place than a station. I suppose you'll be needing a drink, lad? Was it cold on train?"

"I don't feel the cold, Mr Hepplethwaite,"

"You look as if you're dressed for a summer's day at New Brighton. 'Appen you'll need some warm clothes if you decide to come up north. You've heard of Siberia haven't you? Well, we've got places called Oldham and Halifax and Crown Flats at Dewsbury. Coldest spots God made. They make Iceland seem like t'Sahara desert."

"Oh, I'm used to roughing it," said Dai, "I was born in a little colliery village up in the hills, you had to be tough to survive. That's where I learned my rugby, playing it on the slopes of the slag heaps, and not tick rugby either. Proper tackling. It was no place for cissies. I've still got tiny bits of coal stuck in my legs."

"You sound just like the type we need in league," said Joshua whole-heartedly. "It's tough lads we need up north. But let's get some hot tea into us. I wish I didn't feel the cold so much. It's bitter on this ruddy station. On the way in we met a brass monkey looking for a soldering iron."

"I'm dying for a drink too. Come on, I'll buy them." said the welshman leading the way into the station buffet.

At that moment Joshua should have put him on the next train back to the valleys, but fortune telling was not a gift he possessed. Instead he insisted that as he was chairman of the club it was his place to purchase the drinks.

"What will you have lad?" he asked. Joshua had tea or coffee in mind, even Bovril.

"I'll have two pints of best bitter, please, one for the right hand and one for the left. It's an old rugby union custom, look you."

Stanley ordered a pint of mild and Joshua had a large mug of sweet tea. The trio seated themselves close to the smoky coal fire in the dingy refreshment room. Before either of them had got halfway down their respective pots, Dai had downed one pint and was halfway down the second.

"I've heard the ale's very good in the north, Stanley boyo. Which is the best, Lancashire or Yorkshire?" he asked.

"Well, being a Lancky lad I'd plumb for us own ale but in all fairness there's some good ale in Yorkshire too. We've got Boddington's in Lancasheer and Greenall Whitley, then there's John Willie Lees in Owdam; but fair play to 'em, Websters is a good Yorky beer and there's Sam Smiths an all, and they reckon as a pint of Timothy Taylors will knock your 'at off."

"Oh, I'm glad to hear it, you see I've had an offer from Yorkshire. I think I'd better tell you here and now."

"From Bruddersby Stanley lad?" asked Joshua.

"How did you know, Mr Hepplethwaite, bach?"

"News spreads quick, lad, 'appen Hadfield Barnacre's been on to you?"

"Well, there was no mention in the paper, Mr Hepplethwaite. That was our bargain, remember? And when Mr Barnacre rang, well I had to take notice."

"Tha did reet, lad — I'm not blamin' thee. But is the ale going to be the decider or did he offer you more brass?"

"Fifty pound more. But he wants me to play a trial."

"Does he begad? I can understand that with unknown lads but you're an international. And suppose rugby union find out? You're finished then if you don't sign pro.

"I know Mr Hepplethwaite bach, but fifty pounds is fifty pounds. Hang on, I'll get the beer in boys —— have a whisky, Stanley bach?"

"Nay, Bovril for us Mr Powell." said Joshua firmly.

"Tha's not suppin' spirits in day time, Stanley, think on what your Clara said." Joshua wagged a fat demonstrative finger at his scout. Stanley sulked like a scolded child.

"We've got to keep our wits about us, Stanley —— just look at that!" Dai Powell was knocking back a large whisky at the bar.

"I thought you could sup Stanley but this lad makes you look like a temperance preacher. Bloody hell, he's having another pint as well." Stanley wasn't as perturbed as his chairman.

"It'll be allreet. Probably nervous. Dry mouth. Union men enjoy a pint or two."

"This mon looks as if he could sup it out of a sweaty clog," moaned Joshua.

Dai put the tray down on the table. "I've left a whisky on the bar," he said, "I'll just go back for it."

Joshua placed his hand on his face. "May the lord help us, what are we taking on, Stanley? I reckon we ought to forget it."

"First impressions can be wrong, Mr Hepplethwaite. 'Appen you're fearing worst?"

Joshua was the picture of doom and gloom. "I've dropped one, Stanley."

"Open winder then or waft it with thee cap — ,"

"No, crate egg — I've dropped a clanger! A monumental, gigantic clanger!"

"I don't follow you, Mr Hepplethwaite...?

"Don't you? You know that job as I've fixed him up with if he signs?"

"Yeah?"

"It's in a bloody brewery."

Joshua was quite content to sit by the fire and chat. He had no intention of trying to force the player's hand until he had watched his performance for Cardiff against Blackheath. He knew very well that union players were often fish out of water when they changed codes. He had seen it happen so many times. Another lesson he had learned over the many seasons he had been in the game was that it was the unsung players who often made it bigger in league than the top internationals. He would keep an open mind. To try to get a better picture of the would-be league man's background the chairman encouraged him to talk about himself.

"Are you an only child, Mr Powell?" he asked.

"Oh no, Mr Hepplethwaite bach. I've got a brother Keith. Identical twins we are, boyo."

"Not the one that played scrummage half for Neath?" laughed Stanley, "I've sung that song so many times with renegade union lads. It's got some smutty lines in it, has that song."

"That's enough of that, Stanley!" warned the chairman.

"No bach, he's the worst in Wales! Plays in the third team for a minor club."

"It's not everyone's game," said Stanley.

"Oh, but he loves it. He really thinks he'll be a star one day. He couldn't even get in Cardiff fourths so he plays the odd game for this obscure team in the valleys, when they pick him, that is. He's mad to play rugby league."

"Is he by gad?" said Joshua with a grin. "What position does he play?"

"Stand-off, like me. I do wish he had more ability, he's even keener on rugby than I am. We watched a rugby league promotional match in Swansea when we were kids and he's never forgotten it. It's always been his dream to be a big name up north like Jim Sullivan, Gus Risman and Emlyn Jenkins."

"Well, he'll have to be content with seeing his twin brother reach the top," said Joshua.

This was the ideal time to switch the conversation back to the subject of which club Dai should join.

"Was Hadfield Barnacre in touch with you before you left for London lad?" he asked the welshman earnestly.

"We spoke on the 'phone on Wednesday, Mr Hepplethwaite. He's gone on a shooting trip I believe and won't be back 'till Monday."

"Shooting?"

"He's a crack shot, is Mr Barnacre, proper champion at it."

said Stanley.

"I didn't know, tell me more."

"He's a top name in t'north. Clay pigeons and rabbiting, he's represented Yorkshire in big competitions, has Barnacre."

"Well, I'll go to our back privy on a pair o' skates!" exclaimed Joshua. "So that's it!" The penny had dropped.

Stanley gave the chairman a funny look. Joshua hadn't said a word to anybody about the pigeon incident, he didn't want the club being a laughing stock. He decided to change the subject.

"What are we going to do to-night, then? Are you stopping in digs here, Mr Powell.?"

"No, boyo, I've got an uncle Llewellyn here. I'm stopping with him for the night."

"Do you fancy a visit to Jonty Mugglestone's place, Stanley? Mr Powell can fetch his uncle Llewellyn if he wants."

"What goes on there, Mr Hepplethwaite boyo?"

Joshua was on his second mug of hot tea and enjoying his rest by the fire. Jonty's place was one of his favourite talking points, and 'appen by doing so he'd talk Dai Powell round to choosing Lancashire. He knew from past experience that the way to a rugby union man's signature was often through his stomach.

"Jonty is one of Lancasheer's most famous sons. He's on a par with Thomas Beecham and Dixie Dean. A pioneer of great vision is Jonty. A man with a great love for the north of England in his heart and soul. Men like him only come up now and again, a genius. He realised that London can be a cold, unwelcoming place, especially to folk that's never been to the capital before. Lots of northerners come down here —— ferret fanciers, fur and feather men exhibiting their cocks and fowls, brass band men down for contests at Crystal Palace, football fans, and of course Rugby League Cup Final. Where can they go for a good feed? You couldn't go to the Savoy and order a chip butty, could you? Nay. Jonty came up with the answer! It was a stroke of sheer genius! It came to him in a flash. Summat like St. Paul on the way to Doncaster..."

"Damascus, Boyo... I'm welsh chapel you know. Baptist. We had the bible drummed into us." interrupted Dai seriously.

"Well that's as mebbe," said Joshua impatiently, "as I said, he had a brilliant idea, did the lad. He opened a club for northerners right here in the great metropolis, a place where they could be at wom in northern atmosphere. A gradely place where you could put your feet up on mantelpiece and spit in the fire, as they say. It's a little piece of the north set in London; a bit of Halifax and Mytholmroyd all nicely blended, and such grub! Ee, by the cram, you'd not get better in a cook shop... black puddins' from Bury. Boiled, not fried, like ignorant southerners do. Then there's cow heels, trotters, tripe and onions — mushy peas — "

"You're making me chops watter," said Stanley "and don't forget his fried bread, Mr Hepplethwaite. Even my Clara couldn't do it as good. And chip butties that melt in your mouth. A double chip butty and chips, that's his special for colliers, they love 'em —."

It was Joshua's turn to lick his lips. He continued the epicurean praise. "And what about his tatty pie Stanley, by the 'eck? Ee, it's scrumptious, is that, with picalilli and a nice gherkin or two. Then there's Lancasheer hot pot of course. That's what you'll get if you come up to Bramfield Mr Powell, it's best chuck in England. You see, we know how to eat in t'north, it's good healthy grub. None of your rabbit food, like southerners eat — pie and peas, triple barm cakes, drippin' butties, that's real grub — it's good for what ails you is that."

It was Stanley's turn to wax exuberant. "And what about fish and chips, Mr Hepplethwaite? I'm told Jonty got Harry Ramsden from Guisely to coach his cooks how to do 'em proper —— smothered in tomato sauce, that's how I like 'em. I reckon, speaking as an undertaker, with respect of course, that if folks ate good northern grub they'd live longer. I'd lose business, of course —— they reckon as Hollands' pies are good for your love life — our dog's fathered twenty pups and he only gets the gravy —"

Joshua nodded solemnly in agreement. "Do you know, Stanley lad, that Hollands send a wagonette full of pies from Baxenden to Accrington station every morning to catch the train to London. Jonty takes two wagon fulls — not to mention puddins' an' all that tackle. Another favourite of mine is a plate of elder smothered in vinegar followed by a deep fried jam butty. Oh, I almost forgot, a Bramfield delicacy is sweetbreads — you'll love them if you come up, Mr Powell — by the cram, it's mouth watering tackle is that!"

"They do sound tempting, boyo — delicacies from the Orient are they?"

"Nay lad! They're pig's balls. The pig's a wonderful animal, we eat everything but the grunt up north — then there's balm cakes and parkin, chorley cakes and sticky puddin' —"

Stanley butted in with "Mind you, I like a bit of cold hot pot meself, Mr Chairman,"

Joshua nodded sagaciously. "T'left overs fried in drippin's O.K. an all — but you've only got to ask at Jonty's place and they'll do it for you."

"Ee, there's some gradely wenches 'an all, lad! By the cram! They'd fair make you fall in love. Bonny lassies they are..."

Stanley's enthusiastic praise of northern womanhood was brought to a sudden halt by the look on his chairman's face.

"Stanley, behave! Think on! I'm responsible for thee. Besides we've come down here to talk business, not on a wenchin' an' boozin' trip — and if we do go to Jonty's keep your 'ands to yourself. Jonty employs three ex-rugby league hookers as chuckers out — they're reet dirty beggars. One grabs your hair, the other your weddin' tackle, and out you go on the street. Many a lad's been chucked out what's got a bit fresh with the serving wenches and he's blessed the fact it were London and not Oswaldtwistle or Mytholmroyd — it's easier landing down here, no cobbles. Big raw boned Yorkshire lassies they are, built more like forrards than three-quarters — then there's great big dogs what lie about on matting — Watershedding Wolfhounds they call them — bred in Oldham since medieval times for the purpose of keeping marauding Yorkshire tribes from invading Lancasheer."

"Were the tribes wild and savage, boyo?" asked Dai.

"They still are, they turn up in Featherstone jerseys nowadays. But nowt's changed"

"What's the ale like at Jonty's place, boyo?" asked Dai.

" I thought you'd ask that, somehow," said Joshua, winking at Stanley and wagging a finger at the welshman.

"It's match tomorrow lad. Do you sup on a Friday night? It's 'early doors' for t'Rovers' players. I always insist on it. Club rule."

"You can judge for yourself tomorrow Mr Hepplethwaite, I don't think a Friday night drink affects my game. Well, if you don't mind, I'll not accept your offer of a visit to Jonty's place. I'll go out with Uncle Llewellyn instead. He knows a welsh pub where they all sing hymns and arias."

Joshua could tell he had annoyed the welshman with his reference to Friday night drinking. His tone became more formal.

"Very well, Mr Powell. We'll watch the match tomorrow and then I'll report back to my co-directors. That's the procedure. Before you go, have you any questions? Even if you do join our rivals at Bruddersby, don't let it be said that Joshua Parkinson Hepplethwaite didn't extend the hand of help and friendship. Going north is a big decision to make, after all, it's your livelihood and future when all's said and done."

Dai thought hard for a few seconds. "I'm after the best financial deal, of course, and Bramfield and Bruddersby have both promised me employment. It's the change of rules that's worrying me, especially the play the ball business. I can't get the hang of it."

"You will lad," Stanley assured him.

Joshua however was more truthful when he said, "Some

welsh players never learn it proper. We've had some cracking welsh lads but some of 'em never learned to do it right. It's foreign to union men. Any road, why don't I show you how to do it?"

Joshua's suggestion seemed to alarm Powell. "If we're seen together tomorrow the game will be up. Mr Keighley's well known to the lads, even when he wears false beards and wigs. I'd never play union again."

"Nay lad," said Joshua. "I mean here and now."

"But we've no ball," said Stanley, stating the obvious.

"No, but I've a meat pie my wife gave me for my snap on t'train. I didn't eat it so if Stanley lends us his flat cap we'll put pie in it and put this elastic band round it — there we are. Where there's a will there's a way. Now just move them tables, Stanley lad. Make theesel useful, owd prater."

The refreshment room had almost emptied. Dai Powell had left to find his uncle Llewellyn. The refreshment room clientele had been entertained beyond belief by the play the ball tuition; the staff were convinced that they were giving refuge to a pair of northern head cases. Joshua had enjoyed his day thoroughly and the long warm by the fire had done him good. He had just woken up from a nap when Stanley nudged him.

"I think we'd better take us hooks, Mr Hepplethwaite. They're giving us funny looks."

"I wonder why? We've paid for us snacks," said Joshua.

But Stanley insisted. "I reckon we should go. Do you fancy a strip show or a visit to the Windmill theatre, Mr Chairman?"

"No lad. I gave my word to your missus. Besides, I don't want to sit with a gang of blokes in dirty macs watching naked women cavorting. What's use of looking when you can't do owt with it?"

This gem of practical northern philosophy seemed to appeal to

Stanley. He above all people knew there were no pockets in shrouds. He wasn't mean but he was careful.

"Aye, let's save us brass and do a bit o' suppin instead."

Joshua nodded in agreement. "Come on Stanley Lad. Let's get back to the digs. I hope they're nice and warm. 'Appen she'll give us a hot brick apiece for us beds and a chamber pot. 'Appen she'll have a flush lavvy — after all, we're paying eight and sixpence. They know how to charge in London. Come on, . let's hit the town, but behave yourself, Stanley lad. Think on!"

Joshua doffed his hat to the women behind the counter and gave them a bow, the action of a polite northerner to some folks' eyes, but he knew his manners and the sixpenny piece he placed on the tea urn brought a smile to a pair of sour faces.

"That's to show you we're not tight up in the north, ladies. Thanks for the use of your refreshment room as a training ground. If Mr Powell turns pro' you can say as you've done your little bit."

"You're very quiet Mr Chairman. A penny for 'em."

Joshua and Stanley were at Jonty's place sitting in front of a roaring fire eating their chip butty starters, content in the knowledge that a hot brick apiece was in their beds, warming them up back at the digs.

"I'm just cogitating lad," replied the chairman "I'd love to do summat to upset that cocky little beggar Barnacre. Wouldn't I just! The germ of an idea is forming Stanley. First we must see how Powell shapes up tomorrow —— then we'll see. It all depends on how lad shapes."

"Are you going to tell me?"

"No lad, I'm keeping me own council. Hey up, here comes

the grub, lets bidooin' —— by gum, they're big lasses these waitresses. Like second row forrards. By the eck, they'd make mince meat of t'Wigin six."

The two lancky lads needed no persuading, happy to be in a northern environment they got stuck into the food, then settled in armchairs by the roaring fire to listen to George Formby records played on a wind up gramophone. They were in heaven!

Joshua was in a foul mood as they trudged round the streets before the train out to Blackheath for the match.

"By the 'eck, it's crowded in London," he complained.

"'Appen it's market day," remarked Stanley.

Joshua was getting more cantankerous by the second. This stemmed from the breakfast which hadn't suited his northern tastes; the landlady had burned his fried bread, the bacon was floating in baked beans, and his egg was as hard as a golf ball. As if this wasn't enough, she had charged him an extra two pence for his hot brick and threepence for 'the use of the chamber pot'. Joshua pulled his bill out of his waistcoat pocket.

"Insult upon insult, Stanley. I used it three times. That's a penny a pee. She saw us coming did that lass. She must have thought 'aye, aye, here's two gawks what have come up the Manchester Ship on a banana boat, let's put the boot in.'

"Tha's reet, Mr Chairman. She'd a face on her like a hooker's backside - sour as gall. They make jokes about landladies in Blackpool and Scarborough, but they can cook fried bread proper and make a decent cuppa."

The chairman kept up his warlike mutterings about 'bloody southerners' as he entered a newsagent's shop.

"Shan't be a minute, Stanley. Stay theer and don't go off with a strange woman,"

Two minutes later Joshua emerged with a copy of the

Financial Times under his arm.

"Ee, I don't know how you read them sort o' papers, Mr Chairman,"

"I don't lad. It's for thee, part of your disguise. I've got the rest of it in me case. We'll get dressed up when we get to the ground. You can open t'paper and pretend to read it at half-time. You can hide behind it as well. If anyone makes a comment, talk about bulls and bears."

"But I've never been to a zoo - me mam said as I were allergic to elephant fur, so she never took me,"

"Not them kind o' bulls and bears. I mean stock exchange. It's financial talk is that. I am a mill owner, tha knows."

When they got to Lyons' Corner House Joshua said he fancied a cup of coffee. He motioned his scout to a secluded area between the branches of potted palms.

"We're going to make plans now, so keep your voice down Stanley. Whatever happens, nobody must find out that we're a couple of league men."

The chairman's mood mellowed as he listened to the cafe orchestra playing a selection from the Merry Widow, and when one of the girl violinists, dressed up as a gypsy, came over to serenade Stanley, the scout started to get hot under the collar.

Joshua couldn't resist a corny joke. "I bet it takes guts to play that lass!" The joke fell on barren ground.

"No bloody sense of humour, southerners!" he muttered.

When the musicians stopped for a cup of tea, Joshua began his council of war, as he put it. "I'll sit in t'best stand and wear a trilby and a false moustache. You go in the other stand and whatever you do don't engage in conversation unless you have to. Try and look like a city gent. I've got a wig for you and a bushy hirsute appendage and dark glasses. Now, think on, whatever you do, don't ask for black puddin's or meat pies if you go to the bar. And remember, it's not *ale* down here, you ask for *bitter*. Are you with me? Reet, let's enjoy rest o' music programme before we take us hooks for Blackheath."

The visit of Cardiff had attracted a large crowd to the London-based club's ground. Stanley looked as if he had got his disguise out of Dracula's prop box at the local amateur theatricals. He felt a proper berk. Still, it was all in a day's work for a scout. He was deep in enemy territory. He felt like an intelligence officer who had broken through the enemy lines.

His chairman felt just as uneasy in his seat in the best stand. He kept his mouth buttoned tight even when a lieutenant-colonel with an enormous monocle started a tirade against rugby league.

"They daren't send their scouts down this way," he boasted, "I once laid about one of the blackguards with me shootin' stick, don't you know. Damned professional thuggery, that's what rugby league is. Ruining the game in Wales by poaching all the best players. I'd put them all up against a wall and shoot the lot of 'em. Disgrace to the name of Rugby School, don't you know."

The game was a most enjoyable one. Even Joshua had to admit that rugby union could be reasonably entertaining when played by two sides who threw the ball about instead of continuously booting it into the next field. Dai Powell was a revelation. His passing was perfection and in all departments of the game he sparkled; the try he scored shortly after half-time was an absolute gem, and just to rub salt into Blackheath's wounds he kicked a magnificent drop goal from the halfway line. Both Rovers men were highly pleased. They met up outside the ground. Joshua put two thumbs up. "A worthwhile trip, Stanley lad! How did you get on?"

"Oh, alreet, but there were a woman who kept looking at me. I reckon she was giving me the eye - here she is now, Mr Chairman, I reckon she fancies me"

Joshua nearly swallowed his false teeth. "That's no woman! That's Hadfield Barnacre, the crafty sod!"

Chapter 6

Joshua makes his move

It would be hard to imagine the chairman of a present day rugby league club hitching a lift on the back of a brewery delivery wagon. A horse and dray was the transport used for carting barrels of beer about in Joshua's day as chairman of Bramfield Rovers R.L.F.C. The drayman was Bert Brooks who had hooked for the Rovers just after the first World War. Fine snow was falling and the cobbled streets were treacherous under foot as an east wind drove the snow into the faces of pedestrians and draymen alike.

Joshua spotted Fred leaving the brewery yard, fortunately for him the dray's progress was laboured and slow due to the conditions. The hot breath of the horse as it pulled and strained rose like vapour in the rarefied air. The overweight chairman puffed and panted as he tried to keep up with the brewery wagon. He knew it would be making a delivery to the Duck and Dewdrop pub, which was also his own destination. Bert Brooks caught sight of Joshua out of the tail of his eye and he hailed him as he was starting to climb the steep cobbled street known as 'Rattle Alley'. The official name was Pennine Mount but it was hardly ever used. A notorious lodging house, Ada Flanagan's, stood at the very top of the street just before the cobbles gave way to open moorland. The street had taken its nickname from the coughing of consumptive residents of the 'dosshouse'. It was said that the rattle could be heard in the town centre. One of the Rovers' best ever wingers, 'Hairpin Harris', a thin but tough customer, had lived there until the committee fixed him up in digs in the town. Hairpin only lasted a season and a half but even in that short time he had made a great impression in the game. His spindly frame was not made for roughing it and his tackling was almost non-existent, but some of the tries he scored were amazing efforts. When seemingly blocked in by several opponents he could wheedle his way through to the try line and at times his escapology rivalled the great Houdini. The crowd didn't sleep when Hairpin got the ball and in his first season he notched up forty tries. His early life, brought up as an orphan and spending years roughing it on the road and living in doss houses, weakened him and he died at the age of twenty nine, only hours after scoring a ninety yard try in front of his own supporters. Hard-bitten men cried as Hairpin was laid to rest. The killer disease tuberculosis or consumption as it was generally known, had claimed another victim. The disease was a scourge of the industrial north. This was very much in Joshua's mind as he clambered aboard Fred's dray. He could never go up that hilly street without thinking of Hairpin Harris.

'It's a sad old street is this, Mr Hepplethwaite," said Fred.

"Aye lad, it is. There's lots of sad stories can be told about Rattle Alley. But what a season we had when Hairpin scored all those tries. You hooked the ball and he scored the points. "

If poverty ever had a home it would be in this street. It was a thoroughfare of suffering, despair and degradation. The great slump of the twenties had seen once decent women reduced to selling their bodies to keep their families from starving and ending up in the workhouse. Down and outs begging for bread, soup kitchens run by the Salvation Army, women old before their time trudging up the cobbled hill to slave labour employment at the mill. Joshua could never forget the look of hopelessness in their faces and often he had seen a woman faint for lack of food. The 'owd bastard', as he was known locally, who owned the mill refused even to supply lavatory paper. A skinflint who had become rich out of the sweat and blood of his workers. A worker who was a minute late was locked out and sent home — a day's wages lost.

'Th' owd bastard's' mill stood on the edge of the moorland at the very top of Rattle Alley. The old tyrant had long since 'popped his clogs' and the business was run by his sons who had improved the conditions tenfold. Across the moor up a rutted track stood the workhouse — still dreaded as the last place a man and woman's entire family could end up. As a councillor Joshua had fought long and hard to have it closed down but such was the plight of many people that it was still in use. The 'spike' was also situated in the workhouse, a place where tramps could get a night's lodging for a few pence. In the morning they were given the task of breaking stones. Many of the men were incapable of such labour, but the law of the land was adamant that a task had to be completed otherwise the casual could be kept forcibly in the workhouse as a permanent resident. The law had no love for vagrants.

Joshua had made many friends out of the tramps who wended their way up Rattle Alley to the spike. Many of them sold buttons and matches in the street. As the dray ascended the brow Joshua's thoughts went on a trip down memory lane as he huddled in his warm crombie overcoat. A sense of shame came over him as he thought of that warm expensive coat and stark contrasting poverty of those days gone by. Even today they don't live, they merely exist, he thought, as he surveyed the drab soul destroying houses.

Having described the austerity of this notorious area of Bramfield it will surely come as no surprise to the reader to learn that it was the pawnbroking centre of the town.

"Do you remember the song we used to sing as kids?" Josh asked Fred Brooks. Both men burst into song, singing a parody which was very popular in the early part of the century in the north. Sung to the tune of Tipperary, it went:

It's a long way to the pawnshop,
It's a long way to go
It's a long way to the pawnshop,
to the meanest man I know.

Goodbye to your waistcoat
Farewell watch and chain!
If you don't hang on to your trousers
He'll get them just the same.

"I remember pawning me dad's watch and chain at least a dozen times. It were on a piece of elastic, I think, it kept coming back." said Joshua with a grin.

"I've been in a few 'uncles' meself," admitted Bert.

"We were playing Barrow away, back in 1919, and I couldn't travel with the team. I worked in another town so I had to travel from there. The club wouldn't give me the seven shilling for the return fare before the trip so I had to pawn me wife's wedding ring. They don't know they're born today, four pounds ten shillings for an away win, some clubs give. Why, we got three quid if we won away and that had to be in Yorksheer, if it were Lancasheer we only got two pounds ten shillings. Aye, and rugby union players turning pro. for fees of four hundred quid. Why, when I were an amateur in Silloth, Rovers came up and offered me forty quid and I grabbed it with both hands — here we are at the Duck and Dewdrop. What are you doing Mr Chairman, coming to a crummy pub like this? I didn't think a mill owner would frequent a notorious drinking den like this. It's seen more scraps than a wild west saloon."

"Even mill owners have to be born somewhere, Bert, and I was born in this very street."

Bert was amazed at the revelation. "Well, it's a credit to you. You've not forgotten your roots."

"It would be hard to do that Bert — bloody hard for someone born in the very hub of the industrial north. I saw some rum fights when I was a young 'un outside this very pub and do you know, the woman who has it now had it then. There were Irish lads working on the cutting, they'd get stewed then they'd tumble out in the street and start fighting. They loved it. One o' them, a lad called Mick Quinn, played for t' Rovers before your time. A rough 'un, he was sent off so many times for scrapping they had to stop him altogether. Yet a nicer man never breathed. It was the roughest pub in north of England, were the 'Duck'."

"Aye, and its not improved much," said Bert.

It was a well kept secret. Joshua and the Kearsley brothers used the pub as a meeting place when they had something important to discuss. A pub in the centre of Bramfield would have been too public for such a meeting. Besides, 'Owd Sal' the bent old crone of a landlady, who was said to be ninety six years of age, made the best Lancashire hot pot in Bramfield. She was a notorious character who had always done her own chucking out. A kind old soul, she had often given shelter to women who had nowhere else to go. The salt of the earth, as they say in the north. She greeted the chairman with a kiss.

"Well, Josh, old prater, I see that team o' thine lost again at Liverpool. It's gone down plug oil lately. What's wrong lad? Your mates are all in the snug, I'll see as no-one comes in to disturb you. I'll give you half an hour then I'll bring some grub in."

There was a piled up fire blazing in the grate which pleased Joshua. Bob and Bert were already seated in the tiny snug room, looking glum.

"What's up lads, has someone stolen thee wallets?"said

Joshua.

"We're anxious," said Bob."How did you do in London?"

"Did you go out night clubbing?" asked Bert with a wink. Bob gave him a disapproving look.

"I hope Stanley conducted himself in a seemly fashion. He didn't let the club down, I hope?" he asked in a serious tone.

"Did he go off with one o' them destitutes?" laughed Bert. Bob was not amused. Although not sanctimonious like Clara Keighley, Bob was rather straight 'laced' and frowned on suggestive talk. Both bachelors, the brothers were as different as chalk and cheese. Bert was the man-about-town enjoying his afternoon tea dances and having a reputation as a ladies' man.

"Well, did the lad shape, Joshua?" asked Bob.

"By the 'ecky thump. It were great. He's a natural ball player, gentlemen. I've watched many a rugby union chap as you both know, but I've never seen one as impressed me as much."

"But will he make a league player, Josh?" asked Bob.

"I'd bet on it," said Joshua, "first scrum he receives the ball, like greased lightning, he swayed his hips and was away. A grubber kick to the wing and the winger goes over in the corner. Sheer magic. Three tries he scored and made two more, not to mention a drop goal from half way."

"Did you sign him?" asked Bob.

"No. Bruddersby have offered him fifty quid more than us."

The news brought doom and gloom once more to the faces of Joshua's co-directors.

"Have a pickle," said Bob, trying to brighten things up.

"Is he joining them?" asked Bert.

"He might. They want him to play a trial. I don't know when though."

"Can we afford fifty quid more?" asked Bob.

"Definitely not!" said Bert, who held the club's purse strings. "It's out of the question! Besides, we'd have to offer more than Barnacre. Furthermore, we need three more pigeons after that tragedy the other Saturday. Poor beggars shot down by an air gun. I'd give those kids a bloody good thrashing!"

Joshua was determined not to tell the brothers that he knew who the real culprit was. He would have to explain that he had been overheard by one of Barnacre's directors when he was telling the reporters. No, he'd deal with Hadfield in his own way.

Bob had an idea. "I suggest we ask Albert Heneberry to put another concert on. He'll do a show for nowt for the club, will Albert, even if he has to pay the artistes out of his own pocket. He's a good lad."

"That's a good idea," agreed Joshua.

"But what's more important, pigeons or a stand-off? The reporters will have to use public 'phones. Any money Albert makes at concert must go on getting Powell. Are we agreed? It depends on how much time we've got left."

"Agreed!" said the brothers, and Bert added: "You're lucky you didn't watch them at Liverpool, Josh. They played like washerwomen. Dick Glover got sent off. He had a bust up with Porky Davies the big Liverpool prop forrard. It's your turn for 'A' team duty today, isn't it, Joshua?"

"Aye, I know. Don't remind me. I'll be there. Kick-off's at four o'clock. I hate to have to go to Bruddersby and see old Barnacre again. Then we have to play 'em in t'cup an' all — I'm sick to death of 'em."

That same afternoon Hadfield Barnacre was holding a sherry party for the press and a handful of select cronies. If the truth was known, many of them couldn't stand the pompous little chairman. The gentry of the area, the county set, knew him for what he was — an upstart who hobnobbed with the higher echelons of society to further his own ends.

Hadfield had a weakness for good sherry. His nose was always a sure indicator of the amount of the golden fluid he had imbibed. On this afternoon it was bright red. His face by contrast was like an over ripe carbuncle on a plate of cold tripe.

He was fawning over the ladies like the little creep he was. With the clubhouse almost full to overflowing he called for order.

"Well, ladies and gentlemen, and my friends of the press, I'm glad to welcome you to my little sherry party. I am and all. As you will all know, Bruddersby Stanley are having a good season; we've won the last three games on the trot, beaten Leeds at Headingley, and knocked the stuffing out of our rivals Bramfield Rovers on their own midden — I beg your pardon — — ground. The Rugby League Cup first round first leg is nearly upon us. The week after next we are drawn at home to Bramfield and I can tell you we'll lick 'em again, to some tune and all!"

He stopped for a second to acknowledge the polite claps and a few isolated 'hear! hears!'.

"I've got a feeling in me water that it's our year for t'cup! Wembley here we come! Now, here's the news these press hounds are waiting for: this Saturday coming we are at home to Bramley and we are fielding a top rugby union triallist at stand-off. He'll be playing under the name of Jones and I'm told he could be the best buy we ever made. Next week gentlemen, I hope to be telling you that we have signed him on in time for the cup deadline.

"Yes, we are a forward thinking club here at Bruddersby. Only the best is good enough for our supporters. Our 'A' team lads play Bramfield 'A' later on today and we have some fine young prospects, promising lads who will one day be the backbone of the first team. I hope you'll stay and watch the game."

Too polite to tell him to his face, his upper class acquaintances had little time for such an unfashionable game as rugby league, but it was considered polite by them to pretend to take an interest in the club; Hadfield was an influential man and you never knew when he could be of assistance. An hour later the match between the two 'A' teams began. Joshua sat on his own in front of the Bruddersby directors. Hadfield was half-cut on sherry and his bragging knew no bounds. Poor Joshua had to witness his second string get a good hiding. Halfway through the second half the score was thirty three points to seven against the Rovers.

Joshua would never have left a sinking ship in normal circumstances, but when he heard his rival chairman bragging about the appearance of a welsh triallist the following Saturday against Bramley he could take no more. That was it! The idea he had been nurturing in his mind since the London trip now grew into fruition. He'd do it! Why not? Fight fire with fire! That was it. He rose to his feet to leave the stand and, as always, he was polite:

"Good day to you gentlemen. We'll meet again here when we play you in the cup."

"Had enough Josh? You Lancastrians never could take a licking could you?" Hadfield roared laughing at his own joke.

"We're beating Lancasheer at everything at moment. Yorksheer's just beaten 'em at clay pigeon shooting an' all - I were in the team. We thrashed 'em."

"Good for you Hadfield." said Joshua. "I wonder if you're any good at live pigeons?"

Glad to be away from the chaffing of the Bruddersby directors, he made his way to the supporters' club wooden hut where there was a public telephone. He fumed inwardly as he wound away at the handle to attract the operator's attention. To make a trunk call to another town could be a long winded and often exasperating operation. At long last he heard Phoebe Maude's voice which sounded as if it was coming from Russia, not fifteen miles away in Bramfield.

Joshua spoke eagerly into the mouth piece. "Is that you luv? Summat's turned up. I'm at Bruddersby with the 'A' team — what? Oh, we're getting slated — I'm leaving now to drive to Cardiff. I've just heard summat very important. Powell's coming up to play a trial, so I'm off to Wales — yer what? — Oh, don't fret luv, I'll stop at a hotel on way and I'll look after meself, never fear — you've got what? A nice bit o' tripe for me supper? Give it to next door's cat. Ta ra luv."

Chapter 7

Joshua's subterfuge works

On the evening of the Saturday following Joshua's urgent trip to South Wales he was sitting in his armchair waiting for the rugby league results on the wireless. That afternoon Rovers had beaten Dewsbury by thirteen points to ten but it had been a far from satisfactory performance. The half-backs had played very poorly and the language of the crowd was the worst Joshua had ever heard on a ground. They were baying for the directors' blood. One speccy had actually stood in front of the best stand waving his fist at the directors and shouting "Sack the bloody lot of 'em! We want a decent team!" Old Ma' Cornish had threatened Joshua with her brolly and called him "A useless bake!" A noted harridan, at matches she could swear like a bargee and had a repertoire of expletives to make a navvy blush. Bob Kearsley was terrified of her and had even tried to ban her from the ground.

Old Ma' was different again away from rugby league. She was never known to swear during the week and was on the Ladies' Guild Committee at Bob's local church, where he was a sidesman. She treated him with respect when they met on

Sundays but on Saturdays she called him all the names she could think of, and she could think of a lot.

She went too far one Saturday when she clobbered Gus Risman with her umbrella, mistaking him for Jack Feetham a notorious Salford forward who always got the crowd howling at his antics. 'Gentleman Gus' had to have stitches for a cut on his head and Ma' was banned from the ground. Most teams had a Ma' Cornish in their supporters, it all made for colour and atmosphere and the game was the richer for them. These characters, if they were about today, would probably have sorted out the few yobbos who disgrace our game with mindless behaviour and filthy language. Another wonderful character was Mrs Greenall who had two sons who played for St. Helens Recs., a team owned by Pilkingtons' Glass works. Johnny was one of the big stars of his day and it was woe betide anyone who treated him roughly!

"I reckon there'll be some letters in local rag after the way we played today luv," said Joshua to his wife.

"I thought we won?" said Phoebe Maude who could never fathom the mind of her husband.

"Oh aye, we won, but only by a fluke. We should have won by thirty points. The speccies know when we play badly luv and it didn't please 'em one bit. Their reaction was frightening, believe me —— oh good, here come the results."

Huddersfield	10	St. Helens	6
Leeds	44	Liverpool Stanley	16
Warrington	14	Widnes	0
St. Helens Recreation	20	Broughton Rangers	18
Barrow	10	Leigh	10
Keighley	16	Wigan	8
Salford	30	Swinton	6
Batley	6	York	2
Bruddersby	6	Bramley	14
Hunslet	3	——	

"By the heck! That'll do — ee —— turn it off luv! Well — ee — what a result! That'll take the smirk off Hadfield's mush — won't it just! — It's fair given me an appetite for me tea has that. We'll go to the first house at the Hippy afterwards luv, there's a Gene Autry picture on — by the 'eck it's best news ever, I needed summat to cheer me up luv! Let's make a brew lass. Have we any cold hot pot left? Or 'appen a bit of cow heel pie? This calls for summat special to celebrate!"

The following Monday it was back to work for the Rovers' directors. Joshua to his mill and the Kearsley brothers to their building yard in the town. The latter arrived at their office 'early doors' and soon had a fire burning in the grate and a kettle singing on the hob. They were early risers and after they had clocked the workmen in they made tea and relaxed in front of the fire. A news boy pushed a paper through the door.

"Good, here's the paper lad. Throw it over Bert," summoned Bob.

Bob couldn't turn the pages over quickly enough. "Here it is — by the skennin' Nora - by the cram — well, well, well!"

"What the hell's to do Bob?" asked his brother.

"It's the report of the Bruddersby v Bramley game. Listen to this! Pin back thee lug 'oils."

'The appearance of a rugby union triallist in a rugby league game is always a source of great attraction to spectators of the thirteen aside code. Also there is a sense of mystery — an assumed name adds to the excitement; it was no different at Crowbottom Park on Saturday when 'W. Jones' ran out to play at stand-off for Bruddersby Stanley.

'Although the two codes are as different as cowheel and caviar, in many respects the basics of the game are the same. The ball is passed and is caught, players tackle their opponents.

'Jones, however, gave the distinct impression that he had no knowledge of the game of rugby at all. His passing was dreadful and his tackling non-existent, I have never before seen such a poor display, a source of deep embarrassment to the Bruddersby directors who were booed by irate spectators.'

"That's the *Dispatch* — now let's see what the *Herald* has to say — *'W. Jones, the triallist for Bruddersby Stanley in their league game against Bramley did nothing to brighten the afternoon for the home spectators at Crowbottom Park. Rumoured to be a top union star, he wasn't a fish out of water, he was a whale. League is a difficult game to adapt to for amateur players but 'Jones' showed a complete lack of understanding of the game of rugby. Bramley thought it was their birthday as they overplayed Stanley, scoring an unexpected triumph'* — Well, well, that's a blow for big-head Barnacre. I bet he were fuming — I'd loved to have seen his face. I bet the crowd gave him some welly — I'm reet glad we didn't sign him. This has been a lucky escape."

"How right you are," said brother Bert "Joshua must have been watching wrong mon."

Bert Kearsley didn't realise how true his words were. Just then the 'phone rang. Bob picked up the receiver, placing an ear trumpet in his deaf ear.

"Kearsley Builders' Yard. Mr Bob speaking — oh, it's thee Joshua owd lad, what's up? — "

Bert witnessed his brother's face turning puce as he listened to Joshua.

"You — you what?" Bob managed to gulp, "you've signed who? I suppose you've read papers? Words fail me — are you losing your marbles or what Joshua? The man's a ruddy duffer. You what? You're bringing Keighley over here — ? Well, you won't be welcome. I've never heard such stupidity since Stanley Keighley signed the welshman with the wooden leg!"

With that he slammed the telephone down.

"He's bloody well signed Powell," yelled Bob, "and that's swearing by a chap what doesn't swear, but by the 'eck I'll raise biggest stink in t'history of club. I will 'an all!"

"That doctor Joshua went to were reet. He's in need of a rest." said Bert.

"Rest! He needs certifying. It's the action of a prize ruddy idiot - the man's two pence short of a shilling," Bob was on the point of exploding. "And as for that ale can Keighley, he's to blame as well. It were him as recommended Powell in first place."

Bob's face was black with anger as he continued his diatribe. "I'll not serve another week under a chairman who does such unconstitutional things. I'm resigning, I'll sell me shares — not that anyone in their right mind would buy 'em while that Joshua flaming Hepplethwaite's chairman of club and that man Stanley Keighley is scout —Laurel and Hardy could do better."

"Well, let's see what Joshua's got to say first," advised Bert.

"Say, what the hell can he say? He's told me he's signed Powell knowing full well what the papers printed. It's the action of a maniac."

"Don't go on so Bob lad, remember you once had a dicky ticker — oh, here they are."

Bert opened the door. When Joshua and Stanley entered the office a menacing silence ensued.

"What's Keighley doing here?" snapped Bob stiffly at last. "He's not on t'board."

"He's here at my request," explained Joshua.

"Oh, is he?" said Bob, "while you're here Joshua, I want you to repeat to Bert what you told me on the telephone. I reckon he thinks I made it up."

"I have signed Dai Powell for the Rovers," said Joshua without batting an eyelid.

"On your own without consulting us?" queried Bert.

"I already had your agreement, remember?"

"Aye, before we saw today's papers. He made a laughing stock of himself at the trial."

"He didn't play badly Bert," insisted Joshua.

"I told thee he were losing his marbles!" ranted Bob.

"You see, Dai Powell didn't play at Bruddersby on Saturday."

"Yer what?" said an incredulous Bert. "If he didn't who the hell did?"

"His brother Keith. Dai and Keith are twins."

"I can't cope with this," cried Bert, diving into Bob's pickle jar.

"I'll elucidate gentlemen," said Joshua, placing his corpulent backside on an armchair, "Didn't Dai tell us he had a twin who played rugby but was no use?" he asked Stanley.

"Aye, that's reet — you said as you was working on a plan."

"I was an' all. I made me mind up at the 'A' team game at Bruddersby. I decided there and then to use the same tactics as Hadfield Barnacre. I motored to Wales, gave Keith a tenner, brought him up here and put him in a bed and breakfast house ‘till it were time for him to turn out at Bruddersby. I had to keep him out of the way of snooping paper scribes —”

“Well, I’ll go to our Maggie’s weddin’! exclaimed Stanley.

“It were best kept secret of all time, and you never told me, Mr Hepplethwaite,”

“No bloody fear, after the way you blabbed to Crumpsall,”

Stanley pulled a long sulking face. Bob was still mystified by the turn of events.

“What you did was diabolical, Joshua. Do you realise if league got to know we’d be shut down? It’s disgraceful behaviour is that — but by the heck, it were bloody clever!”

The ice broken at last the four men burst into hearty laughter.

“You’re a ruddy genius, Joshua!” exclaimed Bert with genuine admiration. “If that doesn’t beat cock fighting, I don’t know what does. So what’s next move?”

“Dai’s coming up by train this afternoon. I’m motoring over to Manchester then we’re meeting at Piccadilly station. Then we’re going to the Midland Hotel to sign the forms. I’ve notified papers and they seem to think as I’ve gone bonkers.”

“After what they wrote I’m not surprised,” laughed Bert.

“This calls for a celebration, gentlemen,” said Joshua.

“Not more ruddy pickles!” said Bert.

“Nay, whisky.” answered Bert. He opened a cupboard and produced a large bottle of malt. After more praise from the brothers Kearsley Stanley asked if the Rovers would ever be going to France to play again.

“As a matter of fact I’ve had a letter from the club we played. It were Carcassone.” said Bob.

“By gum,I enjoyed that trip.” said Bert. “Let’s go again at t’end of season.”

“We can’t shell out the brass now we’ve signed Powell,” warned Bob, shaking his head.

“What’s brass when all’s said and done? Don’t be a spoil sport — we’ll have enough in the kitty. ‘Appen we might win

cup and we can go be way of a celebration," said Joshua.
"Sometimes you act like Scrooge, our Bob," added Bert.
"Ee, we had a good time, Mr Bert, didn't we just?" said Stanley, grinning.
"Hell fire! Not half! By the heck, we did an' all. There's only one snag, Stanley."
"What's that, Mr Bert?"
"Why, it's language barrier. You'd think as the french would learn language proper, wouldn't you, with them being so near to the mainland? I tried to order pie and mushy peas but I couldn't make 'em understand."
"It's time someone from t'league what can parley frog language went ower to France to learn 'em to talk english proper," said Joshua. "I'll write a letter to Leeds H.Q."
"You mean like one o' them electrocutionists what give you lessons in speaking posh?" asked Bob.
"One of them learned me how to talk proper before I joined t'maisons," Stanley informed them, before reminiscing further.
"Ee, we had a belting time. We went up Ethel Tower and walked down Champions Alice, then we had horse doovres in a pavement caff. At night we went to Follies Bergery and ate frogs legs in aspic —"
"I thought that were near Wigin?" said Bert.
"You're thinking of Aspull," informed Joshua sagely. "I agree it were a good 'do' — I'm all for going again. They were good to us — after all, they are foreigners, you can't expect perfection. They hired a band what played *She's a lassie from Lancasheer* and then we all stood silent while they played the Mayonnaise."
"You can reminisce all you want Joshua, but it will depend on what's in kitty!"
That was Bob's final word on the subject. He then decided to hold a meeting while the three directors were assembled. "I think we owe Keighley here a vote of thanks for t'work he's done in helping us sign Powell." said Bob rather officially.

"Ear, 'ear," chorused his co-directors with gusto.

When Stanley had left Joshua said "I think you were a bit formal calling him by his surname, Bob lad. After all, he is chief scout."

"Aye, but he's not one of us, Josh. He's a paid hand. We have to keep us places. I don't believe in being too familiar tha knows — now let's sort a few things out while we're all here — chuck a bucket o' coal on t'fire, Bert. Now, next Saturday we're away in first round of cup to Bruddersby —"

"Don't remind me," groaned Bert stoking up the fire, "tell us summat we don't know owd prater."

"It doesn't worry me lads. I think we'll fettle 'em," said Joshua breezily as he stuck an expensive Havana cigar between his teeth and contentedly blew out a cloud of smoke. Bob nodded.

"That defeat by Bramley won't have done their confidence any good. Well, do we throw Powell in deep end, or do we give him a run out in 'A' team?"

"Chuck him head first at 'em," advised Joshua. "I reckon as he's a belter. Take a chance, we haven't got a decent out-half any road, so he's bound to be as good as any we can turn out. Besides, they'll be expecting a right puddin, won't they?"

"Right, we'll play him then. We'll pick rest of the team later in week." said Bert agreeing to Joshua's wish. He rustled through a sheaf of papers.

"I've got some costings here — it's about trip to Barrow the following week for the league match. Question is, do we book a charabanc or do we go on train or 'appen walk it now we've spent all the brass?"

"Ee, I'm all for train Bert," said Joshua, "it goes over t'viaduct at Arnside and you get a reet good view of Phoebe Maude's aunty's place. Aunt Betty Ann, they call her, she's almost ninety. Me and Phoebe Maude went there before we was wed — nowt improper tha knows — we was chaperoned everywhere we went, a stickler for propriety is Aunt Betty Ann. She locked me in me room at night. She made a lovely salad for us tea — spring onions fresh from t'garden, cucumber and Webb's prize lettuce, and you shoulda tasted her boiled ham — by the skennin' 'eck! — Ee, by gum, it were good an' all —."

Bob's sharp cough brought him back to the present. "I think our Bert's keen we go on a chara', Josh. 'Appen it'll cost less."

"Ee, I'm sorry lads. I were on a trip down memory lane."

"If we go on a chara' it works out at two pounds and three pence cheaper than it does if we go by train." announced Bert, giving a Joshua a stern look. Bert and Joshua raised their hands.

"We're agreed then, a chara' it is." said Bert. "Now to the question of refreshments after the match. Last year we stopped on t'way back at a little pub and it were reasonable. So shall we do it again? I knocked one and sixpence off the players' wages for the food — are we agreed?"

His co-directors nodded their acquiescence.

"I like a good trip on chara', can I sit next to the driver, Bert?" asked Joshua.

"Joshua Hepplethwaite, you act like a big kid at times," admonished Bert, giving Josh a friendly 'chuck' under his copious chins. Bob handed round his pickle jar and the three directors had another 'shot' of whisky apiece.

"A toast gentleman," announced Joshua, "to our new acquisition — Dai Powell! And to his brother Keith, for being such a bake!"

"To Dai Powell!" chorused his pals in high glee. "And let's hope we give Bruddersby a bloody good thumping in t'cup match!"

"Ear, ear!" was the hearty response.

"We'll have to get a good write up in t'local rag." said Joshua.

"Aye, we will an' all." agreed Bob. "But make sure as they make a proper job of it, Josh. They've got a faulty printing press at *Bramfield Trumpet.* It sometimes doesn't print *h*'s and *e*'s."

"How do you reckon that, our Bob?" asked Bert.

"A few weeks ago they did an article on owd Matthew Briggs' funeral — I've got it in me pocket."

He took out a wrinkled paper cutting from his waistcoat pocket.

"It reads: *'The funeral of Mr Matthew Briggs, Ex-Mayor of Bramfield, was held at St. Peter's Parish church last Thursday. The funeral arrangements by S. Keighley were tastefully and tactfully performed, the late Mayor was mourned by people from several other towns and a beautiful floral wreath was laid on the coffin by the Boy's Brigade, of which he was an ex-officer. He was interned at Bramfield Cemetery and his many close friends walked behind his arse to the cemetery —'"*

Chapter 8

Joshua puts one over Barnacre

Durdock Brearley was one of the hardest men ever to play for Bruddersby Stanley. He would have run through a brick wall and thought nothing about tackling a mad bull. Fear was a phenomenon he had only read about. If Durdock's rugby ability had matched his courage and ferocity he would have been one of the all time greats. As it was he was considered to be a very average player, a utility man who could play anywhere, even hooker. At fourteen stones he was sometimes used by Hadfield Barnacre in the pack, even at prop-forward. His 'A' team appearances far out numbered those he had made for the first team.

Known to the crowd as 'glue pot Brearley' because of his habit of sticking to the ball, he was a muck and nettles bull-at-a-gate type of player wherever he played. Now, at thirty years of age, he was reconciled to being used as a stop-gap player by the club. This season had been his most successful for a long time and for four matches on the run he had played stand-off, his tackling being the nearest thing to grievous bodily harm one could witness on a rugby field. With Bruddersby Stanley on a winning streak he really thought that at last he would be considered a regular first-teamer.

Then came the bomb shell. Mr Barnacre had called him up to the office by way of a speaking tube which connected the chairman's office to the players' dressing room; he was told he had been dropped to the 'A' team because a welsh triallist called 'Jones' was taking the stand-off berth. Naturally, Durdock was upset. While he was playing away for the second string at Wigan, Jones, his replacement, was giving the worst display ever seen by a stand-off on Bruddersby's ground.

When Durdock heard about the debacle he was delighted, even more so when he was assured by Mr Barnacre that he could have his first team spot back again.

It was Tuesday training night at Bruddersby when news came that Bramfield had signed 'Jones', who had turned out to be Dai Powell, the welsh rugby union ace half-back.

The Bruddersby players laughed solidly for five minutes.

"That Joshua Hepplethwaite must be the biggest fool in Lancashire," said Dolly Dolan who had played scrum-half to the welshman. "I've never seen a bigger bake on a rugby field."

When it was announced in the papers on the following day that Powell would be making his debut for Rovers against Bruddersby in the first leg of the first round of the cup, the whole of Bruddersby were laughing.

Hadfield Barnacre made great play of the situation as he entertained his cronies in the golf club. Poor old Joshua was called all the derogatory names Hadfield could think of and the common opinion was that Bramfield's chairman was going 'soft in the yed'.

"By the heck, Durdock Brearley will make mince meat out of Powell," he told his pals, "he were proper annoyed when I dropped him so he'll be ready to smash him to pulp — talk about throwing Christians to the lions! It'll take more than a magic sponge to revive him, Durdock might be a duck egg when it comes to rugby strategy and ball play but there's no more ferocious tackler in the league."

That drubbing by Bramley had really upset Hadfield. He had secretly felt very foolish over 'Jones' performance, but with his arch rival Joshua signing him he felt a lot happier. It would be Joshua who would be the laughing stock. Hadfield was determined to put the nightmare Bramley game behind him and take the first step to Wembley by winning the first leg of the cup tie.

The Rovers team had been very dejected by the poor performance against Dewsbury, the team currently at the foot of the table. After two good seasons the Crown Flats outfit had suddenly hit very poor form and Rovers' captain, Ossie Evans, had expected his team to put thirty points on them. Added to this the news that Rovers had signed on a man who had played an absolute stinker in his trial for Bruddersby further depressed the captain.

The thought of going to Bruddersby was a daunting one, their forwards would be as dirty as they could be and the crowd were like a lynching mob baying for blood. Ossie, tough though he was, shivered at he thought of it. The Rovers team was disjointed, things were not going well, after a very good start the gremlins had got to work and the team had lost confidence. The presence of Dai Powell was hardly guaranteed to stiffen their resolve. Ossie was of the same opinion as Hadfield Barnacre, Joshua was definitely going barmy. Being a discreet sort of chap, he kept his own council, never communicating his doubts to the team.

As they stripped in the away team dressing room at Crowbottom Parade, Bruddersby, Ossie told the lads to ignore last week's match and get stuck in. Being a welsh man, he was naturally concerned about Dai Powell. League was such a different game. Dai Powell didn't seem in the least bit embarrassed by his showing in Bruddersby's colours the week before. Ossie had to admire him for that.

Dai was a cheery soul and the players couldn't help but like this half-back who seemed perfectly at home in the new setting of the paid ranks. What worried Ossie was that he had seen Dai having several swigs out of a pint bottle of pale ale, but he kept quiet about it. He had heard on the grapevine that the new man had been seen drinking in the Bull and Jockey pub the night before. His informant had told him that Powell had supped at least three pints and was last seen walking in the direction of the Railway Shunters' Club.

Already a huge crowd were singing along to Bruddersby and District Fur and Feather Club's Silver Band. A week previously the same crowd had watched Powell give an inept performance. Then they had been amazed and disgusted. This time they were hoping he would repeat the performance. The incident had caused such fun in the town that it was almost a carnival atmosphere which prevailed prior to the game. The ground was firm to hard, the ideal conditions for Durdock Brearley, who loved to crush his opponent on to a hard surface. An expert at the forearm smash (when the referee wasn't looking) he pickled his arms in brine for hours on end to toughen them. He was ready to show that 'nancy' rugby union man what he thought of him.

"They'll be sending a wreath tomorrow when I've done with him," he told his team mates as they lined up ready to go down the tunnel. In the best stand Hadfield and Joshua had already commenced a verbal onslaught against one another.

"We'll make mince meat of thee today, Joshua," said Hadfield in a loud voice, so all the stand could hear.

"Don't count your chickens, Hadfield," replied Joshua.

"Chickens? Your new stand-off's a chicken. By the heck,

Joshua, you've been had lad! Brearley will half-kill him,"

"Aye, I don't doubt he'll try," said Joshua, "and as usual ref' won't do owt because you're on Rugby league Council —"

"I'm not having that! " roared Hadfield, "are you accusing me of bribery or what? Spit it out."

"A chap what shoots innocent pigeons is capable of owt," snarled Joshua. It was out in the open now. Hadfield's face went momentarily white.

"You've no proof!" He roared. At this juncture a tall gaunt man dressed in an astrakan coat and a hard hat stood to his feet.

"Will you be quiet! I've heard about your behaviour and I won't tolerate it! Another word out of the pair of you and there will be serious consequences for your clubs."

A deep silence fell on the stand. The man was Jonah Hawksbody, the secretary of the Rugby League Council. He was noted as a puritanical official who did his job to the letter of the law and a man who had very little humour in him.

Both chairmen knew him well. Hadfield especially was only too aware that anything which brought the game into disrepute angered Jonah Hawksbody and that many a club had experienced his stringent punishments. The two chastened chairmen sat like scolded school boys.

The referee blew his whistle and the game was under way. Rovers' prop-forward caught the ball from the kick off. He ran for several yards and flung a pass to Dai Powell.

Durdock Brearley had him in his sights and immediately flung his bulk at the welsh man. He was expecting to hear the joyous sound of cracked ribs - instead he fell flat on his face. The mercurial Powell had sidestepped and zig-zagged through the Bruddersby back line making a superb opening for Dodger

Dean, who raced down the wing and sidestepped the full-back for a glorious try beneath the posts.

Joshua forgot all about Jonah Hawksbody's presence and danced up and down like a mad dervish. Hadfield couldn't believe his eyes. Durdock felt the biggest fool in the world - the man was a ghost. The Rovers fans roared; deep gloom was the lot of the Bruddersby speccies.

For a short period the home forwards tore into the Rovers six. Fists flew and tempers flared as the Bruddersby pack slowly and relentlessly made ground up the field. When the ball was finally released to the backs the somewhat shaken Durdock dropped it - a good chance ruined. A dangerous dribble by the Bruddersby six almost had the ball over the Rovers line but a courageous dive by Powell saved the day. The home spectators could not believe their eyes. In the best stand people were commenting on the great display given by the stand-off.

"How the bloody hell can he play so well after the bloody awful display last week?" A comment which was silently echoed by all the home spectators. Joshua chuckled uproariously to himself. He'd pulled off some stunts in his time as chairman but this was the best of all! Suddenly little Dodger Dean broke away and Ossie Evans left his opponent for dead with a fine dash to score just left of the posts. This time Joshua hurled his bulk into the air in delight. A cracking sound was heard as the plank beneath his feet was torn from its moorings. After the commotion died down and people had moved away from the gap in the floor, Hadfield yelled "You'll pay for that, Joshua Hepplethwaite!"

"Delighted, Hadfield old trout," said Joshua, "if we fettle thee today it'll be worth every penny."

In fairness to the memory of those Bruddersby spectators who witnessed the cup tie, I won't go into the gory details of their team's demise. Not only was Dai Powell an elusive runner, a fact he proved with several probing runs deep into the heart of Bruddersby's defence, he also tackled Durdock Brearley out of the game. On one occasion he broke from his opponents '25' to place a fine grubber kick for Dodger Dean to score in the corner. In the dying seconds of the game he rubbed salt well and truly into the wound with a craftily taken drop goal. The final score given out on the wireless that Saturday evening was:

Bruddersby Stanley 6 *Bramfield Rovers* 19

The result caused diverse reactions. Hadfield Barnacre called Durdock Brearley the biggest puddin' who ever wore the blue and yellow of Bruddersby; Joshua Hepplethwaite gave each of the players a silver sixpence as a reminder of a great and glorious victory; and Phoebe Maude Hepplethwaite rushed round to the corner shop to buy some of Joshua's favourite boiled ham and a jar of gentleman's relish.

Chapter 9

All that glitters is not gold

The joy in Bramfield was unparalleled for many a year. Suddenly the team had struck form again and the reason was not hard to find - Powell had played a blinder and there was no doubt he was going to be a great acquisition to the club. Joshua noticed the difference in the town immediately on the Sunday when he went to church.

"Good morning to you Mr Hepplethwaite. Congratulations on your new stand-off. Is he church by the way?" asked the vicar.

"Welsh baptist I think, vicar," answered Joshua.

"In that case we'll have to get him a transfer to the Church of England, won't we?"

Life was suddenly light-hearted for Joshua.

"By gum, you've bought a good 'un Mr Josh," shouted an old woman as she white-stoned her step. Only the week before she'd met him in the market hall and showed him up by calling him a half baked moron who couldn't run a chip shop! It was like living on a knife edge, being a club chairman.

Even Clara Keighley wasn't giving her Stanley a hard time. The cup tie victory had been a great tonic to everyone.

Dai started work as a labourer in the barrel house at Ogden's brewery. A nice mannered unassuming sort of chap, Dai soon made friends and enjoyed his work. Especially the free beer. Ogden's had a rule that the workers could drink three pints a day at no charge. It soon became noticed that Dai loved his ale. This surprised many of the workmen who where were under the impression that rugby players didn't over indulge - that is during the day. Everyone knew that some players could sup it 'till the cows came home,' but they usually did it out of the public glare. Not every man at the brewery took his full quota so Dai would often would be the recipient of ale others couldn't drink.

The game at Barrow the next Saturday was another fine victory for the Rovers with Dai again exhibiting his skills. His play making was bringing out the best in the Rovers three-quarters. It was a much happier team that made the long haul back from Barrow in the charabanc. Like most welsh men, Dai had a fine pleasing tenor voice and his rendering of *'Land of my Fathers'* had even the toughest bruisers amongst the forwards shedding a tear. Ossie, the captain, kept his own council. Little Willie Birch, the trainer, had told him on the quiet that he had seen Dai drinking a pint bottle of Ogden's Winter Warmer mild pale ale prior to the game, and when the charabanc pulled in at a pub on the way home he noticed that the stand-off had two pints and two chasers in about five minutes. Ossie was worried. In three days' time they were away again at Salford in a midweek game, then on the following Saturday it was the second leg of the first round of the cup against Bruddersby at Marl Heights in Bramfield. Ossie didn't know whether to have a private word with Dai or not. He didn't want to offend the chap, but he was very concerned that the drink would prove to be his undoing. He would keep his ear tuned in and his eyes peeled on the movements of the stand-off.

"Of all the jobs to put him in a flaming brewery!" he said to little 'Woodbine Willie' Birch as they walked home together after the Barrow match.

The players had been summoned for light training on the Monday evening before the Salford game. Seven o'clock sharp was the starting time, but by seven fifteen there was no sign of Dai Powell. The players had done two laps of the pitch when Willie Birch ran on to the field accompanied by Joshua Hepplethwaite. "A word in your ear Ossie," he shouted to the captain, "Powell's half-cut."

"Drunk boyo? I knew it. You've signed on an alcky, Mr Hepplethwaite."

Joshua stared at the ground. It looked as if all his worst fears were coming true.

"I'm not surprised he's pissed," said Willie, "Me and Ossie knew he was a 'supper' and I've got mates at brewery who told me as he sups as much as he can get."

"Where is he now?" asked the captain.

"I told him to have a cold shower and report for training - look, here he is now!"

The half-back had regained his equilibrium and started on two laps of the pitch.

Salford during the thirties were one of the finest teams in the league. Second from the top of the league, the Rovers players knew that this was probably the hardest game of the season for them. To play away at Weaste was a daunting task. Yes the Red Devils, as Salford were known had a superb back division with Watkins, Risman, Edwards, Jenkins and Hudson all test players.

Joshua wasn't optimistic. They usually got a good hiding at Weaste. He got to the office early on the Tuesday morning. His first telephone call was to Nathaniel Ogden, the brewery owner. Mr Ogden perfectly understood Joshua's concern about Powell's drinking, but told him that every man was entitled to three pints and that was that. But he did agree to Joshua's suggestion that he should send Powell on a dray cart as a second man.

"I'll have a word with Bertie Hancock. He's chief drayman. He's a lay preacher and dead against drinking. I'll give him Powell for the day, if he sees him suppin' any ale at the pubs there'll be a ruction. I'll see as he gets off at half three in time for t'chara to Salford. Leave it to me, Joshua me 'owd brid."

When Dai reported for duty on the Tuesday he started as usual in the barrel house. After half an hour he was called to Nathaniel Ogden's office and told to report to the dray yard where he would accompany Bertie Hancock as second man on local deliveries. By nine o'clock the first delivery was made at the Rat and Robin, next to the abattoir. Bertie was delighted to have a new assistant, but the fact that Dai was a rugby player didn't impress him one iota. He was a new pair of ears to pour his religious sermons into. Most dray men had a free pint at the pubs they called on but all the landlords knew that Bertie never touched the stuff. Poor Dai - never a drop touched his lips the whole day.

Once, when he suggested to Bertie that they had a gill at the Cock and Crowbar, the lay preacher screamed at him: "Look not upon the wine when it is red! It will stingeth like an adder and biteth like a serpent!"

Then followed a half hour's lecture on the evils of strong drink and fornication. Dai was utterly fed up when the time came for him to clock off and walk around to the town hall square to meet the team charabanc. Bertie Hancock had been instructed by the boss to walk with Dai to make sure he didn't nip into a pub or a club on the way. He carried out the task with diligence.

To the newspaper scribes the Salford V Bramfield game had an extra piquance. The prospect of the clash between Dai Powell and Dai Watkins, the two welsh stand-offs, was a very tasty one indeed. Powell had been the current union stand-off up to his turning professional and Watkins was the reigning test man in that position in league.. Added to this was the sudden improvement in form of the Rovers. Joshua Hepplethwaite had further fuelled the interest by stating to the press that this was to be Rovers' year. He had been pictured in the *Daily Dispatch* and *Reynolds News* with his arm around his latest signing. Added to all this, the welsh rugby union had expressed their disgust at the poaching of a top star by the 'northern bandits', as the *Cardiff and District Bugle* described Bramfield.

Furthermore, with the England versus Wales R.L. fixture only three weeks away, speculation was rife that the welsh selectors would pick Powell, even if they had to play him in the centre.

All in all, a cauldron of red-hot interest and speculation was brewing. The Weaste ground was almost full and the booking at Harry Leatherbottom's charabanc company had been very heavy. So much so that Harry had to hire a couple of extra vehicles to accommodate the Rovers spectators wanting to travel to Salford. Leatherbottom's had even brought a horse drawn wagonette back into service.

It was estimated that it would do the fifteen mile journey in just over four hours. A ride on a wagonette was a treat to many older supporters who had never really taken to the modern charabancs. Some of the keen gardeners took buckets with them to gather the horse manure for their rhubarb. It was a well known story in the town that Harry's father, old Ebenezer Leatherbottom, was so mean that he used to charge the passengers a halfpenny a bucket if they wanted to collect his horse's manure.

At the Salford ground the pigeon fraternity had been increased to cope with the extra reporters expected. The match was no damp squib either. The two teams put on a great display of open rugby to entertain the huge crowd. Dai Powell tackled like a man possessed, his attacking chances were stifled by the defence of Watkins, but he impressed the crowd with two magnificent long range touch kicks which had the Red Devils' forwards trailing back to scrum down on their own line. Joshua and the Kearsley brothers were delighted to see the general improvement in the Rovers' play. Dai Powell's presence had

Rovers supporters about to leave for the match at Salford. A keen gardener is intent upon filling his bucket with horse manure before he climbes aboard the waggonette.

inspired Ossie Evans who was turning in some of the best performances of his professional career. With five minutes to go Rovers were leading eight points to six to the astonishment of all concerned. With a minute left on the clock Risman, that master tactician, called for the ball. With superb judgement he slotted a drop goal from the half way line. A draw eight points apiece. Far from being downhearted, the Rovers players were in ecstasy. From the best stand, Joshua was gazing down at the scene. He had never seen his players in such a happy mood for ages, team spirit was high and the mood in the stand matched the mood in the arena.

The Rovers directors shook hands with all and sundry, ignoring the advice of their parents who had told them never to shake hands with strange men! Bob Kearsley started to sing his favourite hymn '*Onwards Christian Soldiers*', which was taken up by the Rovers supporters in the stand. The North of England has always been a bastion for religious fervour. Suckled no doubt by the stringent tradition of sending children to Sunday School, so it was of no surprise when this fervour broke out in the most unlikely places. At many rugby league grounds it was common to hear the crowd singing hymns. The St. Helens directors had caused quite a stir back in 1929 when they sang hymns on the dock side at Southampton as they waited to welcome Hutt, Hall and Hardgrave. Hymns were ideal of course, there were sad ones for defeat and happy ones for victory.

Rovers directors singing a hymn before the match at Salford.

Joshua sat back in his seat pulling on a large Havana cigar and surveyed the scene. As the feathered fowl took to the air to carry reports of the match to the different newspapers, the flapping of their wings was a pleasant sound to his ears. They always reminded him of the doves of peace out of the good book he had read at Sunday school. Somehow it was a reassuring sound. It made him feel at one with the world. He hadn't felt so contented and well for a long time. He could certainly look back on the events of the last few weeks with pride and pleasure. The league had been taken by storm by the signing and, even more satisfying, he'd defeated Hadfield Barnacre's side. The prospect of whipping them again when they met in the second leg of the tie on the following Saturday was an appetizing one. The good news had been somewhat dampened by the way Powell had been hitting the bottle. It was something that mustn't get to the press. The players present at the training session had all been sworn to secrecy. Stanley Keighley was his only worry. A couple of jars could easily have him blabbing the tale all over town. The scout was on his last warning, another indiscretion and he'd be out on his ear. Joshua was sure he wouldn't risk that. A definite source of comfort was Nathaniel Ogden's cooperation. He hoped the brewery boss would make the welshman a permanent assistant to Bertie Hancock. At least it would keep him off the ale during the day. Joshua planned to take Nathaniel out for a meal to talk the situation over. They had to keep Powell off the ale. He'd do it if he had to go to every pub and club in Bramfield and ask them not to serve him.

Life was never easy, he mused. Here he was with one of the hottest properties in modern day rugby league, but at the same time saddled with a chap who could sup three times more than a navvy. Still, despite that, things were looking up. The speccies had more respect for him —

"Penny for thee thoughts, Joshua, me owd tater pie,"

Bob Kearsley's question broke Joshua's reverie.

"I were just day-dreaming, Bob. Thinking over events, tha knows." said Joshua.

"It's been a hectic week or two," said Bob, reflectively.
"I hope as Powell will keep off the bottle. I think as we can cope with him,'' replied Joshua, aware of Bob's point.
"Aye, I should hope so and all," said Bob, who could be quite sanctimonious when the mood was upon him. "We don't want ale cans playing for t'Rovers. It's always been a God-fearing club. You think we can sort him out then?"
"I'm confident we can, Bob lad," But the truth was that Joshua wouldn't have put money on it.

Hepplethwaite's mill was working at full pelt, Joshua had captured a couple of very nice orders from a provincial fashion house. In business and in sport the outlook was decidedly better than it had appeared several week's before. Just when everything in the garden is rosy the gremlins usually strike to remind us mere mortals that fate has the last say. As the mill clock struck three thirty on the Friday afternoon it was one of those moments. The 'phone rang. Hyacinth Grimshaw, Joshua's secretary, took the call. "It's Mr Nathaniel Ogden for you, Mr Hepplethwaite,"
The office telephone was one of the earliest models invented and had to be wound up before the speaker could be heard distinctively. It sounded like an aeroplane taking off. These early 'phones caused the speaker to yell rather than talk in a normal manner. Eventually Joshua could hear the caller and he bawled down the speaking tube:
"Joshua speaking — I've been going to ring you Nat to invite you out for a bit o' dinner — you what? — he's done what? — — by the 'eck, he's done it this time... it's big cup tie tomorrow an' all... thanks for ringing Nat... aye, keep him theer out of anyone's road. I don't want press finding out. I'll be right round."

"What on earth's the matter Mr Hepplethwaite?" asked Hyacinth anxiously. Joshua had no secrets from his secretary. He knew she was tight as a clam when it came to private information.

"It's our star half-back, Mr flaming Powell! He's paralytic drunk at the brewery. It seems he was alright on Tuesday and Wednesday when he were acting second man on t'dray. Today there were no deliveries so he starts suppin' in t'barrel house. He's as drunk as a coot according to Nat Ogden - stoned out of his mind!"

"We'll have to get him out and sober him up then, won't we Mr Hepplethwaite...? Let's see, we must be discreet ..." Joshua loved having a university educated secretary. She was well worth the five pounds a week he paid her, well above the average.

"By gum, you're a good lass Hyacinth - always cool in the darkest hours of mortal combat. You're reet, we must be discreet. Them two reporters are staying at the Frog and Monocle. They were hot on my heels for snippets of news this morning when I went up to t'ground to talk to the groundsman. If they get to know we'll be in Dicky's Meadow. Proper ruthless these reporters are, give 'em an inch 'an they take a hundred miles. It seems I've signed on a chap what's got a drink problem - and to cap it all he works in a brewery. Can you see the headlines? Can you see the laugh on Hadfield's face? By the heck, Hyacinth lass, I'm finished if this gets out."

Joshua put his face in his hands and almost sobbed. Hyacinth acted as she always did in such situations. "I'll make a nice cup of tea," she said. As she mashed the tea in the office kitchen her mind focused on her employer's dilemma. She would have walked through fire and brimstone for him. She knew how he worried. Something had to be done. All of a sudden she had a brain wave.

"I've put a stick in it, Mr H," she sang out quite cheerily, "and I've solved the case of the inebriated half-back. It sounds like a

Sherlock Holmes thriller doesn't it? Cheer up Mr H., all is not lost."

Hyacinth had never been to a match in her life but she loved the Rovers. Besides her mill secretarial duties she often wrote letters on behalf of the club and dealt with rugby league business.

"Solved it lass?" asked her boss eagerly sipping his whisky-stiffened tea. Joshua's face was dark with worry, and his hand shook. "If you can come up with something lass I'll give you a half crown bonus."

Hyacinth put a Craven A in her long holder and typed away as she cogitated. "If we send a car someone could easily spot Mr Powell in his inebriated state," she explained logically, "so why not get Mr Keighley the undertaker to go in his funeral car? Put Mr Powell in a coffin and people will think it's just another dead body. What do you think?"

Joshua perked up immediately. "Classical lass! Get him on t'phone for me!"

Fortunately Stanley was having a cup of tea at home when the club chairman rang. "Stanley Keighley, undertaker and rugby league scout. Can I be of help?"

"You can drop the formalities lad, it's me, Hepplethwaite. Get off thee backside and get round to the brewery pronto. I'll take a cab and meet you outside the maggot yard at back of Pat Flanagan's ferret farm in Clogmorton Street. I'll be wearing me false beard and wig, so watch out. Say nowt."

"What's up Mr Chairman?"

"Never mind what's up - just do it. Think on. Say nowt. Come in your hearse and put a coffin in - shift thee sen'. You're future as club scout depends on this! Thinkon!"

The plan went without a hitch. Joshua wasn't noticed as he stepped into Stanley's funeral limousine clad in his disguise. At the brewery Dai Powell was flat out in the barrel house. They were told he had been drinking since early morning. Nat Ogden told them that he had given the workmen a tanner apiece and an extra pint of ale to keep their gobs buttoned. It was news that gladdened Joshua's heart. Powell was placed in the coffin and carried out to the limousine.

An errand lad on a delivery bike was the only person to witness the rugby league player being placed in the hearse. Stanley had made sure the lid was firmly on the coffin. The lad stopped his bike and stared "Who's dead, mister?" he asked.

"The bloke in the coffin," answered Joshua.

When the nosy lad had cycled off Stanley took the lid off so Dai Powell could breath. Joshua peeled off his disguise and scratched his head, wondering what to do next.

"Where to now, Mr Chairman?" asked the undertaker cum scout.

"That's the million dollar question," replied Joshua.

"We can't take him back to his digs that's for sure. Mrs Murphy is dead against booze, she wouldn't have him in the house. We must keep it hush hush, the less folks know of our movements the better. All our clandestine peregrinations will be to no avail if anyone finds out."

"I were just on t'point of saying same thing, Mr Chairman," said Stanley. Then he added "We've got to keep it in t'family, so to speak. Let's go to your 'ouse,' appen Mrs Hepplethwaite would understand."

"Nay, you don't, Stanley, she'd divorce me. She'd do a lot for the cause would Phoebe Maude, but she wouldn't give shelter to a drunken man. Tell thee what, we'll go to your house - turn to t'left at Woolworths' corner and be sharp about it."

"Our Clara will kill us - nay, have a heart Mr Chairman."

"I thought thee were a Rovers man through and through, Stanley Keighley? Would you desert a sinking ship?"

"I am, I mean I wouldn't... but there are limits..."

"No buts about it ... lets get him theer."

He indicated the left turn in the brew with a wave of his thumb.

"What the 'eck will I tell Clara? You know she hates drink."

"That's as mebbe but we'll put her to the test, won't we? If she's as devoted to t'Rovers as she claims then she'll help us sober him up and get him in a decent state for the game tomorrow. Anyhow, going to your house won't raise any eyebrows, neighbours are used to corpses coming and going. If we took him in at my house folks would be lifting coffin lid to see if they knew the departed corpse. They're a nosy bloody lot."

Stanley shook his head and tut-tutted to himself. He wasn't enamoured by the idea at all. Clara got quite rampant when she started on intemperate behaviour. He shivered at the thought. The chairman's voice broke upon his anxious reverie.

"Stop at corner shop Stanley - I want to get summat."

Joshua returned with a small parcel. "It's what's known as a peace offering Stanley. When white hunters go on safari into deepest regions of unexplored Africa and them foreign parts - and I don't mean round 'Uddersfield way either - they take beans and trinkets to give to the cannibal king and his concubine."

"Isn't he a cricketer? I saw him once when he played in Lancashire league - West Indian test player he were."

"It were Constantine, you daft bat. I was referring to king's women folk. To pacify them they took gifts. That's what this is, a gift of a box of chocolates to pacify your Clara. I take it she isn't against chocolates as well as ale is she?"

"Ee, by gum, no she's a proper sweet tooth is Clara. I reckon as that's a good move, Mr Chairman."

Joshua tapped his head. "Being a chairman of a club is summat like being a general, Stanley. You have to apply stratagem. In charge of the situation at all times. A modicum of subterfuge doesn't come amiss, either. By the heck, these cobbles are bloody bumpy..."

At that moment there was a gurgling noise from the coffin.

"By the heck, he's been sick! He'll make a ruddy mess. I've only borrowed this limousine, it's not mine. I'll have to clean it up now." exclaimed Stanley.

To add to Stanley's concern, the stand-off started to sing.

"*Sospan Bach...*" he bellowed. They were almost at number ten Arkwright's Sidings as luck would have it. This was Stanley's house.

"Reverse quickly Stanley!" yelled Joshua.

"Drive up back ginnel and on to the coal tip. Your neighbours might be used to corpses in coffins but I doubt if they've heard one singing before."

The half-back then gave them a few lines of *David of the White Rock* just to add to their panic. Joshua had always loved a welsh tenor voice but not on this occasion. Especially when he started on a well known bawdy union song.

"If I was a marrying man sir and thank the lord I'm not sir, the kind of girl that I would wed would be a scrum-half's daughter... all together boyos!... *Oh, she'd...*"

Joshua had flung the hearse door open just in time to ram his hard hat over Dai's mouth and staunch the flow of vocal putrefaction.

"Stopped him just before he got t'mucky part... what a ruddy mess we're in. I told thee when we were on t'station in London as I had a feeling in me water about Powell. Fancy signing on a piss head. We want talking about, me an' thee. Well, we can't stay here all neet. I think he's gone back to sleep now. Drive on. Let's face the music."

"I hope you haven't smothered him with thee bowler," said Stanley anxiously.

"It might be best solution come to think of it. And a bit of extra business for you." said Joshua.

In fact Dai had gone to sleep. Stanley left the lid off the coffin and placed a cushion under his head so that he could sleep peacefully. It was impossible to see through the windows so the two Rovers men felt safe enough for the moment, although neither felt happy with the situation.

When Clara opened the front door to let them in they were

met by an aroma most pleasing to the nostrils.

"By the 'eck, Clara love, that smells reet good," said her husband appreciatively.

"It's only a bit of scrag end and a few onions. I've made us some chips as well. You're welcome to stop, Mr Chairman Hepplethwaite. There's enough for three." Joshua accepted Clara's offer.

"Thanks lass. It's Phoebe Maude's knitting club tonight. They do it for the Clog and Stocking fund and the raggy arsed school... begging your pardon Clara... by gum, it smells reet tasty 'an all. You can't beat a northern lass when it comes to cooking good grub."

When Clara had left the parlour Stanley whispered to Joshua. "I thought your missus' knitting club were on a Monday night?"

"It is. I had to pretend. Pull the wool over her eyes, it's no harm. It were only a white lie."

Stanley started to laugh.

"What's up?" snapped Joshua.

"You're a caution, Mr Chairman. Knitting, pulling wool... it were reet clever were that."

Joshua pushed the scout into the armchair.

"It were an unintentional pun, crate egg. This is no time for facetious merriment and flippant jocularity. A crisis has been thrust upon us."

"When are we going to tell her?" asked Stanley. At this juncture Clara came into the room with a saucepan full of scrag end and placed it on the table.

"What are you whispering about? Is owt up? I don't like whispering. It's secretive and clandestine, so the vicar says."

"Nay, lass, of course not. By the gum sticks, that looks like best scrag end in Northern Union, does that Clara."

To emphasise his praise for Clara's culinary expertise, the chairman parked his ample posterior on one of her best parlour chairs and got stuck into a pudding dish full. As they were eating the scrag end stew Joshua was aware of a clicking noise.

He could tell from Clara's face that it was annoying her as well. She could stand it no longer.

"Stanley lad, will you do summat about that top set o' thine? It fair grates on my ears. Why don't you get a proper dentist instead of wearing teeth what's been passed on to you?"

"What did you say, Clara lass?" asked Joshua. "What do you mean, *passed on?*"

"O.F.D.s Mr Hepplethwaite - other folks' dentures. Terminology of the funeral business." she explained.

Joshua was horrified. "I've heard of folk making their own but not wearing ones that have come out of mouths of dead corpses."

"It's standard practice, is that," said Stanley, "one of t'perks, tha' knows. Some folks like to show their appreciation when I've laid their loved to ones to rest with the taste and decorum that befits 'Keighley' Funeral Emporium and House of Retirement'. Sometimes it might be a ring or a watch or 'appen a jock strap. I've had the odd gold tooth as well. It's par for t'course is that. You've heard the expression dead men's boots? Well, I've got scores of pairs, all sizes. What size do you take Mr Chairman? 'Appen I could do you a pair for a couple o' shillings, seeing I know you."

"You've opened my eyes, Stanley. But false teeth I can't stomach. It's proper ghoulish is that. You're nowt short of a necromancer and a grave robber." Joshua shuddered at the thought. Stanley only laughed. "You're too nesh Mr Chairman. I always wash the teeth first. Several folks have said they've had better fitting top and bottom sets from me than they've had from t'dentist."

"Tell me no more Stanley, you're turning me stomach!"

The sound of a dog barking distracted Stanley's macabre thoughts to more earthly things.

"It's Clara's Aunt Polly's dog. It's one o' them alligations. Give it some scrag end, Clara lass. Aunt Polly has had one o' them women's operations. An hysterical rectum, they call it."

When Clara left the parlour Stanley said. "We'll have to tell the lass soon. Suppose Powell wakes up and starts singing again? He'll raise the whole street, then we'll be up shit creek and no paddle."

"Leave it to me. I'm more diplomatic than thee." said Joshua, helping himself to more meat and onions. He was working on the condemned man theory, a good feed before the drop. As soon as Clara was seated again the chairman said "Clara lass, me dear old mam, God bless her, always said tell the truth and shame the devil. I'm sure as you'll agree, being church."

"I do of course, Mr Hepplethwaite. Your mam were right." agreed Clara, in a serious tone of voice.

"Well then, there's a chap outside in Stanley's hearse and he's blind drunk. Can we bring him indoors?"

Clara stared at Joshua for several seconds before replying. She was dumbfounded and scandalised.

"You what? Do my ears deceive me? Any man worse for drink has no place in God's house *or* mine. I'm a God fearing woman. My father were a sides man at St. George's for forty year and his father before him. Strong drink never passed their lips. On me uncle Fred's side were a temperance preacher called Rev. Brimstone Bagley who spent his whole life waging war on the evils of John Barleycorn and spirituous liquors. All me own life I've tried to live up to his teachings and you come here into my house and ask me to take a drunken man in. You've scandalised me, Mister Hepplethwaite..."

"Reet, lass, that's enough!" interrupted her husband who could see that Clara was warming up into a full blooded tirade on the evils of alcohol.

"So much for your diplomacy," he added.

Clara thought hard for a second or two. "He isn't dead is he?"

"Nay lass, dead drunk," said the chairman.

"Well, he's not coming in. Dead yes but not drunk. What would folks think?"

"And I thought as you were a Rovers supporter lass. You tell folk as how you watched 'em when you were a kid." said Joshua.

"What's that got to do with it?"

"There have been many crises in Bramfield Rovers' history Clara. I assure you that this is one of the worst."

"I don't follow thee, Mr Hepplethwaite lad?"

"The drunken man is our new stand-off, Dai Powell. and we want him sobered up and fit for tomorrow's cup tie. Are you with me?"

Clara was staggered. "But vicar told me as how you've told him he was a baptist. A welsh 'un at that. They don't drink. Are you sure it's him?"

This annoyed Joshua. "Sure, of course I'm sure. You look at life through rose coloured specs, lass. There's a rotten apple in every barrel. Baptist or not I tell thee as he sups ale and owt else that's going. Facts are facts. Powell is a boozer. Now will you help us?"

"What will vicar say? It's the devil's work is this."

Joshua was getting more cross by the minute. "If Powell doesn't play tomorrow, Clara Keighley, the vicar *might* have something to say. He's a die-hard is the vicar, and he's no saint either. I heard him give the referee a mouthful at Featherstone. And it wasn't biblical language either, I can tell you."

After more thought she said "He can go in t'coffin shop. He'll be quite comfy there."

"Won't it be cold?" asked Joshua.

"'Appen it will, none of Stanley's clients have ever complained."

Joshua looked at Stanley. The undertaker studied the signed photograph of Alf Ellaby on the wall. Both were at a low ebb.

"Alreet," said Joshua at last. "I reckon as we've no choice. Let's drive him round the back, Stanley. 'Appen we can put a hot brick in t'coffin to keep him warm."

"I'll put one in 't oven, Mr Hepplethwaite,"

"Thanks for nowt, Clara," said Joshua under his breath.

Powell was still supine in the coffin, as is the way of a corpse. With a bit of powder on his face he could have passed for one.

"It's like Siberia in here, Stanley," complained Joshua, shivering.

"A coffin shop has to be cold. Mr Ramsbottom over there's about at right temperature for committing to the earth."

"You mean as there's a dead body in here?"

"Course there is. It's a coffin shop, not a chip shop."

Joshua was a courageous man but he didn't feel at home near corpses. "I'm fetching doctor." he said.

"It's too late, Mr Hepplethwaite, Mr Ramsbottom's dead, I can guarantee that."

"Not for him, you berk. For Dai Powell. I'm ringing Dr Bradshaw, the club doctor. We've got to confide in him and take his advice. I'll go and use 'phone."

"Don't forget to leave a penny on t'mouthpiece."

"You should have been a Yorksheer man. Talk about 'never do owt for nowt'." Half an hour later the medical man arrived.

As luck would have it Dr Bradshaw was an ex-army doctor and very much to the point. "The fellow's drunk, blotto, Hepplethwaite! What the bloody hell is going on?"

Joshua told the doctor the background to the story. "There's only one way, Hepplethwaite. I can't sober him up. I'll knock him out and when he wakes up in the morning give him lots of black coffee. It's damn cold in here, have you no heat, Keighley?"

"Go and see how that hot brick is going on Stanley," ordered Joshua. "Wrap it up in one of your socks."

Dr Bradshaw pulled out a lethal looking hyperdermic and pulling down Dai Powell's pants gave him a shot in the buttocks. "Stay with him, Hepplethwaite, do you hear? Don't leave him. It's hardly likely he'll will wake up, but if he does the shock of finding himself in a coffin and all alone could give him a heart attack."

With a military click of the heels the doctor departed saying,

The club doctor gives Rovers stand-off an injection in Stanley Keighley's Coffin Shop.

"Remember, Hepplethwaite, lots of black coffee - with a bit of luck he'll be fit to play, and keep him warm!"

It was a good fifteen minutes before Stanley returned. What with the extreme cold of Keighley's burial establishment and an inherent dislike of such places, Joshua was at his wits end when the chief scout did at last return.

"Where the hell have you been, Stanley?" he demanded angrily.

"I were heating the brick, Mr Chairman,"

"I thought as you'd never come. You're always in the lane when you should be in the field, Stanley... now put brick in t'coffin and put lid partly over him... that's reet, now you're shaping. You can keep him company now, I'm off to get your Clara to make us a hot drink. I'll bring thee one back."

It was a long night. Light snow was falling which was a worry to Joshua. What if the tie couldn't be played? On second thoughts, he mused, it might be a good thing - if the game was cancelled Dai Powell wouldn't have to turn out. Try as he could Joshua couldn't sleep. Wrapped up in his thick crombie overcoat, as well as four coats that had belonged to Stanley's clients, the cold was still intense.

Stanley, on the contrary, was sleeping like a baby. Dai Powell was out to the world. The injection had certainly worked.

"I should have got Dr Bradshaw to give me one as well," said Joshua to himself when a rasping fart shattered the eerie silence of the grim emporium. It was of the classic mould.

"Was that thee, Stanley?" called out Joshua, startled.

The acute report had rocketed the undertaker back to wakefulness. "Nay, I were asleep - was it thee?"

"Course it wasn't. If it were me I wouldn't be asking if it were thee. Use your brains. It must have been Dai Powell. 'Appen he's waking up."

"Nay, it weren't Powell," Stanley assured him, "it were from far corner."

"Who the hell else is in the place?"

"Mr Ramsbottom."

"Mr Ramsbotttom? I swore you to secrecy. There's only me and you and Dr Bradshaw that knows about Powell being here. Do you mean to say as you've babbled to someone else? Who is this bloke, any road?"

"I showed you him before. He's a corpse. Have you forgotten, Mr Chairman?"

"You mean...? Nay, it were of this earth were that. It would win prizes."

"I tell thee, it were Mr Ramsbottom!" Stanley was getting very testy.

"It were somebody's bottom, that's for sure. Don't tell me as we do it when we're dead? Are you sure we're alone, Stanley?"

"There's only thee and me, Mr Hepplethwaite,"

"Aye, and when I gets me shoes on there'll only be thee."

"Don't panic Mr Chairman. It's only a corpse. You get used to them; they're my bread and butter."

"You're welcome to it, with jam on," said Joshua.
"But I forgot, you're married to one, aren't you?"
"You mean my Clara?"
"Of course I mean her. Who the hell else are you wed to?"
"I'll admit she's a bit dull and she does go on a bit..."
"A bit? She were injected with a gramophone needle, were that lass... I don't know how you put up with it. You can't swear, can't drink, you can't read paper unless she's vetted it first in case there's owt mucky in it, you can't break wind... life's not worth living. How do you go on for you-know-what? Man to man Stanley, tell your uncle Joshua. It's no marriage is yours, is it? Come clean lad... wink wink... I bet you're a veritable monk."
"My cousin was a venerable monk in Yorksheer."
"Not venerable, veritable. It means genuine, like what it's supposed to be."
"Anyway, I'd take odds on you being almost celibate. You know what I mean...?"
"I don't Mr Chairman."
"It begins with an *S*, Stanley,"
"Oh, semolina pudding, you mean? It's me favourite is that... oh, I get it regular. One thing about Clara, she can cook."
At that moment another roll of thunderous flatus burst upon their eardrums with staccato-like intensity.
"It's only Mr Ramsbottom again," explained Stanley, in a matter of fact tone, "It's par for the course with dead bodies up to three days."
"I've had enough!" cried Joshua. "The Hepplethwaites have been warriors and explorers in their illustrious history but they've never gone in for dabbling in the unknown... where the bloody hell is the latch? I'm off. I'd sooner meet Frank Whitcombe down a ginnel on a dark night than dabble with tackle like you have in here, Stanley."
Sensing the whereabouts of the door in the dark he hit it with his shoulder. The Hull K.R. pack couldn't have done a better

demolition job. It flew off its hinges and brought down a chest full of brass coffin handles on top of the chairman. To make matters worse, Joshua had forgotten about the snow and fell flat on his backside. Next door's ginger tom cat set up a hell of a din and before he knew what had happened he was confronted by an old woman in a long night shirt brandishing a poker. Fortunately she recognised him.

"Is it you, councillor?"

"Aye, Sarah, it's me - I were just having a nocturnal constitutional and I slipped on the snow. Goodnight, lass."

Joshua didn't go home. He had already told Phoebe Maude that he wouldn't be returning so he made his way to the club house at the ground. He let himself in and shuddered at the silence that greeted him. He climbed into a basket full of players' jerseys and stockings and contented himself with the thought that anywhere was better than Stanley Keighley's coffin shop.

Chapter 10

A miraculous resurrection

Compared to Stanley's coffin shop, the kit room at the ground was like a heated greenhouse. Situated next to the boiler house, it was always warm. Consequently Joshua had succumbed willingly to the call of Morpheus and had slept like a new born baby. Waking up in a basket of jerseys was somewhat of a surprise but he soon realised that it was vastly more appealing than the macabre impedimenta of 'Keighley's House of Rest'. He picked up a corner flag and made his way down the players' tunnel onto the pitch. A wintery sun was creeping its anaemic way through the clouds, a very thin dusting of snow was falling but the ground appeared quite green. Joshua had to admit to himself that he was disappointed. Normally he would have been delighted that the threat of heavy snow had been averted by a thawing wind. He felt guilty about such thoughts, but a cancellation would have meant that his precious stand-off Dai Powell would have chance to sober up. "Blast the lad!" said the chairman to himself as he made his way up the embankment and across the cinders to the gate. What on earth was he going to tell the speccies? He'd be drawn into a web of deceit and deception and he didn't like it. He'd have to spin a yarn, he couldn't announce that due to being pissed Dai Powell wasn't fit to play.

There would be hisses and boos when the lad went round the field with the board which informed the speccies of any team changes. It wasn't unknown for irate spectators to attack the directors. "Who the heck in his reet mind would be chairman of a ruddy rugby league club?" he said to himself out loud.

His musings were interrupted by the voice of Fred Noblett, the groundsman. "By the 'eck, Mr Chairman, couldn't thee sleep? Has wife put thee out? I thought thee were a prowler."

"I were just checking pitch, Fred. I stuck a flag in t'ground and it were quite soft. No frost."

"It'll be a decent day for t'match," Fred assured him. "It'll just suit Powell, I'm hoping he'll turn it on. It's great to have a decent out-half again." The remark gave the chairman acute butterflies in his stomach.

As Joshua negotiated the slippery cobbled back streets in the vicinity of the ground, he was greeted very pleasantly by supporters who shouted complimentary remarks instead of the usual rude comments he was used to hearing.

Delivery boys on bicycles greeted him like a favourite uncle at Christmas, butchers swilling the sawdust from their shop floors yelled at him jovially. "You're doing a great job, Mr Hepplethwaite," cackled an old shawled woman who was polishing the kerbstone outside her terraced house.

"You've got a smasher in that new stand-off," was one remark which did not set his heart on fire. By the time he'd reached Arkwright Sidings he was sick to death of the name Dai Powell. He dreaded to think what was waiting for him at Stanley's house.

The clamour of the town hall clock made strident demands on his ear drums as it noisily declared to the Bramfield townsfolk that it was eight o'clock. An angry man opened his bedroom window and yelled "Belt up! Don't they know it's a Saturday?" before closing it with a crash.

Clara Keighley, however, was wide awake and busy white stoning the front door step as she warbled *"What do you give a nudist on his birthday?"*. Joshua was in two minds about making his presence known to her, he was very careful where

Clara Keighley was concerned. She was as unpredictable as the Bramfield speccies. But Clara was full of warmth and sunshine.

"Mornin', Mr Hepplethwaite!" she sang out friendly enough, her crabby mood of the day before completely gone.

"No need to go round back. Mr Powell and Stanley are having their breakfast in t'parlour. You're welcome to join 'em."

"Are they be gad!" whistled Joshua in disbelief.

True enough, Dai Powell was tucking into a large plate of fried bread, dripping butties and warmed up hot pot. He gave Mr Hepplethwaite a welcoming smile.

"Good morning, Mr Chairman bach. Grand day for the match, boyo."

Joshua didn't reply; he couldn't. This was miraculous. At last he managed to say "Are you feeling alright then?"

"Never better, boyo! I've never looked forward to a game as much as this one."

Joshua was dumbfounded. Dai had consumed a pot of tea so it was no surprise when he had to go outside to the lavatory.

"Watch them flags Dai lad - they're slippy. We don't want you breaking your ankle." sang out Stanley.

"Have I been dreaming, or did all that happen yesterday?" asked Joshua when they were alone.

Stanley grinned. "He must be as tough as old boots. He woke up at seven o'clock as if nowt had happened, did a couple of laps of the block, then started suppin' tea and had his breakfast. He's as fit a fiddle, is the lad."

"Bloody remarkable," said Joshua, helping himself to a cup of tea. "Last night he were as tight as a drum."

"I reckon as we should box very carefully, Mr Chairman. Say nowt. Let's count us blessings that he's O.K."

"You're right, Stanley. Keep mum if he mentions it. But it can't go on, tha knows. My nerves won't stand it, I've got terrible waterworks problems as it is and worry only makes it worse. I'll end up in a straight jacket if we don't sort it out. We can't keep it hushed up for ever, lad."

"Let's get today's game over first, Mr Chairman, then 'appen you could have a chat with club quack. 'Appen he'll know of a cure for Powell's addiction to alcohol."

Their whispered conversation was brought to a halt by the half-back's return. He was the picture of health. "I'm rarin' to go, boyo! I'll see you later, I think I'll go into town."

Joshua was horrified. "Nay, nay — lad! I want you at t'ground —— we're having a pre-match pep talk and I want to get some information about you. It's for a special booklet we're bringing out about t'history of the club." Joshua was lying though his teeth.

"Very well, Mr Chairman, if you say so, boyo,"

"Eleven o'clock sharp, Dai lad. Think on!"

Joshua breathed again. Another bender and Powell would be too drunk to turn out. It was like treading on eggs. *Something had to be done.*

Bramfield town centre was a hive of activity. Saturday morning was always busy, especially on match day. The folk of Bramfield loved fresh air, little wonder when most of them either worked down the mine or else in the claustrophobic hustle of a noisy mill. Those who could would take to the hills but in the winter time the pull of a rugby league match would keep most of the men folk in the town. After all, the match would have been the talking point of the whole week, culminating in the excitement on the Saturday of two teams battling it out. Player or supporter, rugby was a man's game. Soccer was for softies and tennis for cissies. That was the way of thinking in northern rugby league strongholds like Bramfield, Oldham and Keighley.

A Saturday had a carnival flavour. Many colourful characters came to the town, all of them out to make a bob or two. The visit of rivals Bruddersby Stanley for the second leg of the cup tie was bound to bring a large crowd to the Marl Heights ground. Even for an 'A' team game, the Rovers usually drew two to three thousand spectators. For today's tie ten thousand were expected to attend.

Stunt men and buskers were a big attraction in the streets, while the more mundane street hawkers sold matches, moth balls and jumping beans. Most of these characters lived in local doss houses. 'Potato Pete' was a regular visitor. His act was to throw large potatoes high into the air and crack them open when they landed on his bald head. Another star performer was 'Alf Hignett, the Bradford Houdini'. His wife would secure him in chains then invite male members of the crowd to try to break them open. No one ever could. After five minutes groaning and grunting Alf would break free and immediately go round with the collection box.

Outside the market hall was a waste ground used for the open air market. On a Saturday it was the favourite place for bookies' runners to stand while colliers, often still in their pit black, would play pitch and toss while a 'look out' kept his eyes open for an approaching policeman.

Such was the scene as Albert Heneberry, the Supporters' Club chairman, led a gang of cronies towards the Canal Vaults. They were in great spirits as they sang and shouted "Up t'Rovers!" waving their ribbon festooned rattles above their heads. A casual passer-by could have been forgiven for thinking that a Chicago style gangster was at large with a machine gun, such was the staccato ear piercing din made by the rattles.

A party of Bruddersby supporters smothered in the club's colours of green and yellow gave the V sign and blew wet raspberries, but it was all good hearted stuff. Besides, it was only a fool who would cause trouble. It was well known that Bramfield bobbies were big men who didn't mess about. Policemen on the street were respected in those days.

At the Canal Vaults rosette sellers were peddling their wares. The talk was all about Dai Powell.

"He'll be best in whole league, will the lad," said Albert.

"Only been in game a week or so and he's held his own with

Dia Watkins. I saw Fairclough of St. Helens and Johnny Greenall of the Recs., but I reckon as this lad will be just as good, if not better."

The ale flowed and before long a sing song was in full swing.

"Who's going to give us a solo?" bawled Albert, above the hubbub.

"I'll sing," shouted a thin chap with a brown moustache who answered to the name 'Ferrety Fred."

"Give us '*the tune the old cow died of*, Fred!" yelled one of his mates. "Nay, I'll give thee '*A bird in a gilded cage*'." said Fred.

"You can't sing that!" shouted Albert, suddenly gripped by panic. Fred took no notice and piped up with the famous ditty.

"She's only a bird in a gilded cage,
a beautiful sight to see,
you'd think she was happy
and free from care
she's not though she seems to be.
It's sad when you think
of her wasted years
for youth cannot blend with age
her beauty was sold for an
old man's gold
she's a bird in a gilded cage!"

Eli Hawksley, the owner of the pub, was busy pulling pints and his young wife Miranda was serving pie and peas. It was common knowledge in the town that Eli was approaching sixty, while Miranda was in her early twenties. The marriage had been the talk of the town and Eli the butt of a cartload of jokes. Albert knew how easily upset he was, so when Fred began to sing he watched the landlord's face intently to see what the reaction would be.

The song, always a great chorus number, was taken up by the entire pub. Albert had not worried in vain. Eli's face was as black as thunder and poor Miranda was crying bucketfuls into the pie and peas. Eli always did his own chucking out, this was the age of tough landlords; being an exwrestler helped. Poor Fred, who didn't know he had caused offence, was lifted off the floor, propelled over Eli's head, and thrown through the swing doors into the street.

The onlookers could not have seen a finer performance in the Saturday cowboy film at the local flea palace. Poor Fred was seeing stars and wondering what on earth he had done wrong while a passing policeman kept himself aloof, knowing full well that Eli Hawksley was quite capable of keeping law and order in his own 'boozer'. Albert felt like apologising to Eli and his wife but decided that silence and a speedy getaway would be more suited to the occasion. Such incidents were not uncommon in Bramfield pubs and neither was the scene which greeted Albert and company at the tram stop. Old Ma' Cornish, the villain of the popular stand, was forcing herself onto a tram with the aid of an umbrella, for all the world like a Zulu warrior on the charge. Albert smiled to himself. It was a typical match day.

A roar greeted the Rovers players as they ran onto the pitch. The band were playing '*The entry of the Gladiators*' and the spectators were fired up with excitement at the thought of another great display by their team.

It was the Bruddersby pack, however, who hogged the limelight for the opening quarter of the game. They had come to wreck the Rovers six, that was obvious from the kick off. They punched holes in the home team's defence but completely ignored their three-quarters who were itching to get in on the action.

"I'll drop lot of them next week. They're sticking ball up their jerseys!" roared an irate Hadfield Barnacre as he watched his bullocking forwards battering away on the Rovers line. As so often happens, it was the team on the receiving end who scored first. At last Dai Powell handled the ball from a scrum won by the Rovers pack. Jinking, he beat his opposite number and easily sidestepped the full-back. The popular stand erupted and the terrace was a sea of cap throwing, delighted speccies. The best stand rivalled Bedlam as the home fans stamped their approval on the floor boards, much to the anxiety of Bob Kearsley who worried himself sick about the stand caving in.

The visitors knew that they were fighting a losing battle and their pack, noted throughout the league as a dirty lot, threw caution to the wind and lashed out with fists and boots whenever the chance allowed them. Fury was building up in the popular stand. Steam was visibly rising in the cool air and a casual observer might have pondered on how much was due to the anger of its occupants. The language on the terraces was not fit for the ears of maiden aunts as Bruddersby tried to knock the excreta out of the Bramfield forwards. The visitors' backs could well have gone home. It was a war of the big men. It only needed a swinging fist by 'Dirty Dan' Postlethwaite, the visitors' second row star to start trouble. Dai Powell received a ball on his own line. He hoisted a kick to clear but was immediately clobbered by Postlethwaite with a punch Joe Louis would have been proud of. Old Ma' Cornish was over the fence in a flash; her mate 'owd Tosh' Bott followed her wielding his walking stick. In seconds Postlethwaite was subjected to a beating, Ma's umbrella lashing him like a scimitar in the hands of a marauding Persian. The referee's whistle shrieked, two huge bobbies raced across blowing their strident mouthpieces. To compound the fracas, opposition players traded punches and a riot seemed imminent as speccies poured over the rickety fence onto the field.

Despite the pandemonium, the second row man managed to hear the referee giving him his marching orders. Like an obedient kindergarten child, he meekly left the field breaking into a gallop when he saw the two old codgers in hot pursuit. Ma Cornish was caught by one of the bobbies and forcibly removed down the players' tunnel. The fury of the home speccies was still at fever pitch when minutes later the visitors'

Rovers supporters break onto the field to chase Bruddersby's Dirty Dan Postlethwaite who has been dismissed by the referee for an 'early bath'.

hooker cross-buttocked Dai Powell and followed up by kicking him in the shins as he lay writhing on the grass. Again the referee had no compunction about despatching him to the dressing room. The half-time whistle was sweet relief to the referee who knew that he was the luckiest official in the rugby league not to have a full scale brawl and riot on his hands.

For once Hadfield made no comment. Out of politeness Joshua invited him to the club room for a brandy, but he just left the stand and didn't return for the second half. He was humiliated.

It is not for me to rub salt into the Bruddersby wounds, they were a pathetic lot as with two men short they tried to staunch the flow of tries which followed as the Rovers ran amok. Dai Powell helped himself to two more and the final aggregate score of the two ties read Rovers 58, Bruddersby Stanley 10.

Suffice it to say, the ale flowed like water in Bramfield that night. Victory was indeed sweet.

Chapter Eleven

Revenge is sweeter

The reverend Ronald Bucktrout was in particularly jovial form at the ten o'clock Sunday service at St. Helens on the Hill parish church. Situated on the summit of a Pennine foothill the church was the recipient of bitterly cold winds carrying ice lodging in lofty crags. It was said in the town that the vicar was allowed an extra five pounds a year in his stipend to purchase long johns and thick vests. It was not the extra cash that was making him smile on one and all, neither was it the unusually mild weather, the reason lay in the presence of a portly gentleman in a crombie overcoat who was sitting in a pew below the pulpit.

As the rev. Bucktrout wound up his homily he gazed upon his corpulent parishioner and smiled benevolently.

"Now, dear brethren, it is my pleasure to mention something we won't find in the good book. I refer to the game of rugby league, although I'm told on good authority that Featherstone Rovers approached David after his amazing triumph against Goliath — but he wouldn't give up his amateur status." Those who got the joke tittered politely. Those who didn't sat stone-faced.

"—— Quite —— ahem — I see in front of me Mr Joshua Hepplethwaite - it would be hard not to see him - sorry, my little joke, don't you know - our worthy chairman of Bramfield Rovers R.L.F.C. Well done Rovers! The double triumph over our - I won't say hated, that would be unchristian - our detested (well, let's be honest, we don't like 'em do we?) rivals Bruddersby Stanley has warmed the cockles of our townsfolk. The Rovers are on the road to Wembley once again. My congratulations Mr Hepplethwaite."

As the chairman left the church he was greeted by "Well done, owd lad," and "God bless you, Mr Hepplethwaite cock," until he was embarrassed and began to blush. It didn't need the vicar to tell Joshua that the directors were the toast of the town. It was an amazing state of affairs. To please the Bramfield speccies one had to be a magician and a prophet with a modicum of miracle worker thrown in for good measure. The club's capture of Dai Powell, the welsh wizard, had really impressed the supporters. The three directors, who, normally, according to general opinion, couldn't run a chip shop, were suddenly the best thing since Fuller's Earth. Joshua wasn't fooled by this unusual show of adoration, he was well aware that it was a success built on quick sand. Things could just as quickly turn the other way and once more the directors would be the recipients of insults, angry letters in the paper, and snide remarks in the street.

But, as Phoebe Maude kept reminding her husband, the supporters were praising the board so why shouldn't he enjoy it? "Why be glum, owd lad?" she said as she poked her podgy fingers into Joshua's bag of sticky Owd Betty Plant's Winter Mixture.

"It can't last, that's why,"

"But nothing ever does love,"

"'Appen so, but when you know what I know and have seen what I've seen you'd be worried too. Powell has an illness love. Alcoholism. I reckon the lad's gone past the point where he could stop."

"'Appen he might, Josh. Stranger things have happened at sea love, let's keep us fingers crossed and he might pack up when he sees the folly of it. I mean, it's not affecting his play, you've said yourself he's a belting stand-off."

"That's reet, love, best in Northern Union as me dad used to say, but that's the tragedy and all. You see, no athlete can perform up to par when he's hitting the bottle. His form will deteriorate and his rugby prowess will go into steep decline."

"'Appen, love, but don't take on so. Have another sweet. They're reet soothing. I'd have a word with the doctor if I was you Joshua."

"I've made an appointment, love. Eleven o'clock tomorrow morning."

Phoebe Maude put another bucket of coal on the fire and blew it up with the bellows. "They're nowt like a reet good soak, I'll bring thee a basin of warm water with some mustard in and you can bathe your feet. It's most comforting thing out is that, then I'll get dinner ready while you have a nap. It'll do thee a world of good lad." She bent over and gave Joshua peck on his forehead.

"By gum, I got a good 'un when I got you, lass,"

A tear rolled down Joshua's flabby cheeks.

Such wifely affection coupled with the comforting tranquillity afforded by the mustard bath and the blazing fire soon had the chairman rocked in the arms of Morpheus.

One would have thought that such placating of the savage breast would have resulted in sweet dreams. On the contrary, the chairman's somnolent fantasy took the form of an uneasy and disturbing near-nightmare which was peopled by little men in number six jerseys running around with whisky bottles in their hands. One had a leek sticking out of his left ear while another with blood shot eyes was filling one of Stanley's coffins with bottles of pale ale. The coffin was then rowed down the Styx, the river which waters the hot lands of hell. Joshua woke up with a start, shivering.

On the Monday morning he still felt very worried. He hadn't slept well and his old water problem was playing him up again.

Even on the short walk to the doctor's surgery he had to pee three times up back ginnels.

Doctor Bradshaw told Joshua bluntly that he could do nothing to help Dai Powell unless the player himself wanted to stop drinking. Joshua knew that Powell did not consider that he had a problem. The doctor did, however, come up with an idea which appealed to the chairman. He had heard wonderful reports about the power of a monk at Mount Melleray in County Waterford in Ireland, who treated alcoholics.

Father Brendan, the guest master at the monastery, had achieved a reputation for wheedling dipsomaniacs away from the bottle with a combination of devoted kindness and simple logic. His method was to give the amount of liquor to which the sufferer was accustomed, but in reduced quantities every day until at the end of the cure, he was drinking water. It was said, however, that it was the moral influence of the monastery that pulled the man through in the end.

"Sorry I can't be of more help Hepplethwaite, but there's one thing you need to do immediately,"

"What's that doctor?"

"Why, take him away from that bloody brewery, of course!"

Joshua's next port of call was Mrs Murphy's boarding house where Dai Powell was in digs.

"I was expectin' you, so I was," said Mrs Murphy when she opened the door. "I'm sorry to tell ye as Mr Powell's as drunk as the divil, so he is. But then I'm sure you know he's a wild one for the bottle."

"I do an' all, lass, and I'm very sorry as you've got the problem of coping with it. Can I see him?"

"Sure ye can, but be careful. Me own husband, Murphy himself, took to the booze, so I know what it does to a man. 'Tis a curse, so it is."

Mrs Murphy's announcement didn't surprise Joshua, but only served to deepen the feeling of desperation that had come upon him in the last week. Bitterly remembering the hope he had felt when he had gone down to London to sign Dai, and the great joy of the fabulous victory over his arch rival's team, Bruddersby Stanley, the experienced rugby league chairman went at the welshman like an aussie prop-forward.

"Morning Dai, I suppose you're feeling a bit worse for wear? Well lad, I've no sympathy for you. You've got the ability to be the best stand-off in the history of the game. You've done my heart proud this last few weeks, the way you've played. The team's in great spirits. They're good lads, all o' them, but none of them's got you're class. But the way you're going on you're letting the team down, and me who put his neck on line to get you, against the better judgement of some, I might add," referring to the Kearsley brothers, "and not least but last, you're letting yourself down."

Despite getting his words mixed up a bit, Joshua's off-the-cuff speech seemed to have hit home. Dai looked at his chairman and blushed, his initial aggressive reaction subsiding as he realised the truth of what he had said. His hands shaking, he looked at Joshua and said "I'm truly sorry, Mr Hepplethwaite, I always thought a few pints didn't do me any harm. It never seemed to affect my play. I got used to drinking after my shift down the pit back home, and all the players at home drink like fish. It's expected, boyo. Thats union boyo''

Joshua looked at the sullen looking welshman, and thought how his attitude had changed since that first meeting at the station in London. Then Dai had seemed almost offended when Joshua had admonished him for drinking the night before a game. At least now the player accepted that boozing too much was bad for his game. Joshua then outlined the plan he and Dr Bradshaw had thought up; giving up the job at the brewery and working at the ground, and even going to Ireland for a 'cure' if he needed it.

But Joshua was no mug. Talk was cheap, as they say, and Powell's promises of amendment didn't fool him one iota. The Kearsleys agreed with Joshua that the only action would be to put him on the transfer list if the drinking continued.

The problem would be to keep the news of his addiction from spreading throughout the league. Already, whispered remarks were being made in the town about the new lad being a 'piss artist'. In fact, several landlords, on the directors' instructions, were doing their best to see that he didn't have one too many. Such a situation was like a festering boil, it had to come to a head.

The week following the great victory at home to Bruddersby, Rovers played Barrow at Marl Heights in the league and again put on a superb display with Powell stamping his authority on the match with two tries and a couple of drop goals. A week later at Wakefield he was given a wonderful ovation by the home speccies after yet another fine display. He was the find of the year.

Joshua was beginning to believe that Powell was genuinely trying to defeat his problem and he had heard encouraging reports from Mrs Murphy. Her welsh lodger was staying sober. He had started work at the ground and appeared to be enjoying it. The directors were delighted.

The following Saturday the club were due to entertain the mighty Huddersfield in the second round of the Challenge Cup. The men in the claret and gold usually beat the Rovers but this time the Rovers were going to put it across the men from Fartown. In pub, club, and corner shop the talk was about the forthcoming game, the drudgery of work in the mill and down the pit was relieved by the pleasing prospect of a Rovers victory.

Dai had seemed in great spirits when Joshua had called at the ground on the Wednesday. He had talked about the mouth watering approaching cup tie with enthusiasm, the idea of meeting the all conquering Huddersfield seemed to hold no fears for him. That evening the team were going to have an extra training session and Joshua had called a special meeting of the board to discuss ground improvements. As the directors watched the players filing on to the field for training it was suddenly evident that Powell was missing. After a quarter of an hour, 'Woodbine Willie' Birch informed the directors that he had received word that Powell was blind drunk back in his digs. Mrs Murphy had found him lying on his bedroom floor.

A council of war was held behind locked doors. In whispered tones they agreed that another clandestine trip in Stanley's limousine was called for. The undertaker was only too glad to help, much to the joy of the directors, in fact he told Joshua that his wife had quite taken to the welsh lad and would put a bed up for him in the parlour. Doctor Bradshaw was informed and when Joshua and company reached Powell's digs he gravely informed them that the only course was to wash him out with a stomach pump. The local hospital was out of the question. In next to no time the news would be all over town. The only course of action was to take him to a private clinic known to the doctor. It was a very weak and chastened footballer who awoke the next morning. After a breakfast of cold milk he was lifted into the funeral limousine and driven to 10 Arkwright Sidings. To avoid the glare of nosy neighbours the car was driven to the back of the premises.

"I don't approve of strong drink tha knows and I don't normally admit drunkards to this 'ouse," said Clara in her best sanctimonious voice. "However, seeing as it's for t'Rovers, I'll make an exception,"

She made a bed up for him by the fire and fed him with cups of warm milk. "He'll not play on Sat'day, Mr Chairman," announced Clara when Joshua returned to check on her charge. "I've seen better looking corpses in Stanley's coffin shop."

"Then we'll have to act quick. Can I use the 'phone Clara lass? I've got to tell the *Bramfield Trumpet*, they go to press today. It's better to tell 'em so the speccies will know before the game. There'd be a riot if we put it on board the lad takes round before the match —— we're in Dicky's Meadow Clara lass. It were a bad day when you're Stanley spotted him."

"Are you blaming my husband?"

"Nay lass, nay. Only —— well, your Stanley does seem to pick 'em doesn't he? That bloke with the wooden leg he signed and ——"

"I'll thank thee to shut thee gob Mr Chairman —,"

Joshua was saved from a tongue lashing by a cry from the 'patient'.

"Give me a drink, boyo —— I'm as dry as a stick —— "

"Give him lemonade," suggested Joshua.

"We haven't got any but I'll find summat,"

"All reet lass, I'll come in the morning. Me and my co-directors are holding an emergency meeting to discuss this mess."

The news that Powell would miss the Huddersfield game hit the fans hard. It hit his team mates even harder. The gallant Rovers went down by twenty points to ten. What is the point, dear reader, of saddening you with a litany of what might have been?

On the following Monday the papers announced the bombshell news that Powell was on the transfer list at £750. The reason given was that the player was unable to settle in the town and wanted a different job. Suddenly the directors were prize idiots once more. Angry gangs gathered on street corners, a brick was thrown through Joshua's parlour window. Ma' Cornish lambasted Bert Kearsley with her umbrella when she met him in the street and even poor old Stanley Keighley was greeted by boos when he pulled up at the cemetery in his hearse.

When Joshua arrived at the Keighley's house the next day he could see that Stanley and Clara were having a flaming row.

Stanley shouted. "Thee bloody great crate egg Clara! Fancy

giving him aunty Mary Alice's home made wine — have you got nowt between your ears lass?"

"It's harmless, you daft crow," she yelled back.

"Harmless. It's bloody lethal stuff is that, and you've given it to an alcoholic."

"It never did aunty Mary Alice any harm...,"

Joshua didn't stand on ceremony. He barged straight into the parlour. "What the 'eck's going on?" he demanded.

"He's spewing up in lavvy," explained Stanley.

"She's been feeding him raspberry wine and now he's sick".

"All reet, let's hear the full story. What happened, Clara?"

"Well, it were like this, Mr Hepplethwaite. After you left yesterday I gave him water because I hadn't got any pop, then he dozed off and slept like a lamb all night long by the fire here. I didn't move him, we put more coal on t'fire and he were like a bug in a rug ——"

"All reet, get on with it lass," said her husband impatiently.

"Well, this morning, Stanley went off early to see a corpse what wanted committing and I made Mr Powell a cup of warm milk but he wouldn't have it, he started yelling for whisky and beer. Well, I were afraid the neighbours would hear him, so I gave him a glass of aunty Mary Alice's home made wine. It's vicar's favourite and mine 'cause we're both teetotal, and much to my surprise he liked it. Well, I gave him a couple more glasses and then he started singing them welsh songs and then he sits up and puts his hand on me knee. If it had been any other man I'd have slapped his face but seeing it were for 'cause of the Rovers I didn't bother. Then he sang a love song to me and said I were best thing since Aphrodite. Who were he, Stanley?"

"Alfred Hiti? I think he were a Maori prop forrard who played for Batley"

"Was he hell as like!" corrected Joshua, "Aphrodite was the Greek Goddess of love. She were a wench"

"Bloody hell, he must have been pissed!" remarked Stanley.

"Then what happened?" enquired the chairman.

"He wanted more wine but he'd supped it all so I found a bottle what were on back shelf in the kitchen. There was lemonade in it."

"What colour was it?" asked Stanley who had suddenly turned very pale.

"Lemonade colour of course - white. Anyhow, he supped it then he made a dash for t'closet. He's been there ever since."

"No wonder lass. Do you know what you gave him? That were my embalming fluid."

After dinner on the Monday of the stunning transfer news Joshua sat in the club committee room waiting for the telephone to ring. He wasn't disappointed. Six clubs agreed to pay the full price for Powell. There was no haggling. The Kearsley brothers joined him in the late afternoon eager for news.

"Well, has owt happened?" asked Bob.

"I've sold him," answered Joshua.

"For t'full fee I hope," said Bert.

"Nay, I were offered full fee by six clubs, including Wigin and Hull, but I took an offer of £700 instead."

"You did *what*?" cried an incredulous Bob.

"Oh, don't worry, Bob, I'm putting the fifty quid in myself to make up the full fee."

He peeled off ten large white fivers and laid them on the table in front of his co-directors.

"I always knew thee were barmy Joshua Hepplethwaite. Now I'm convinced." said Bob touching his head to indicate that Joshua was a candidate for the lunatic asylum.

"And may we ask who bought him?" he continued sarcastically.

"Certainly," said Joshua.

"A Mr Hadfield Barnacre of Bruddersby Stanley."

A tear of laughter ran down Bert's face.

"You're a bloody rum 'un!" said Bob. "Have a pickle, or 'appen revenge is sweeter!"

END